MINAW'S CAVE

Minaw's Cave

Jeannie Thompson

iUniverse, Inc.
Bloomington

Minaw's Cave

iUniverse books may be ordered through booksellers or by contacting:

iUniverse
1663 Liberty Drive
Bloomington, IN 47403
www.iuniverse.com
1-800-Authors (1-800-288-4677)

ISBN: 978-1-4759-8699-0 (sc)
ISBN: 978-1-4759-8700-3 (ebk)

Library of Congress Control Number: 2013907075

Printed in the United States of America

iUniverse rev. date: 04/18/2013

CONTENTS

PROLOGUE

In 1839 Ephraim and Mindy Humphrey brought their three children, Andy, Addie, and Desdemona, from Georgia to the Cherokee Indian Territory capital of Tahlequah. They built a home, established a mercantile, and found their place among both their white and Cherokee neighbors.

When an epidemic of measles struck, Mindy helped her neighbors but in doing so she brought the disease into her household, an act that cost her life and that of little Desi. Ephraim turned to alcohol to cope with his loss, and Andy took over operation of Humphrey's Mercantile.

Andy eventually married Annie Price, daughter of the Methodist minister. Addie trained to become a teacher and kept Levi Ballew, who wanted more than friendship, at arms length. They all looked to their future as Tahlequah, the young settlement that was the capital of the Cherokee Nation, began to grow.

1863

Ephraim and Mindy Humphrey
(Deceased)

Andy	Addie	Desdimona
(m. *Annie Price*)	(m. *Levi Ballew*)	(Deceased)

William (19)	Humphrey (14)	
Jackson (19)	Josephine (Josie) (12)	
Hazel (14)	Evan (10)	
Delphia (12)	Melvina (Melly) (9)	
	Nicholas (5)	
	Baby D (Susie) (3)	

CHAPTER 1

INTRUDERS

October 1863

Sounds of wagon wheels crunching across gravel carried through dense underbrush to the cabin that sat where the trail dipped below the hill. Addie knew within minutes she would hear sounds of horses' hooves and the squeaking of leather saddles as the mounted riders accompanying the wagon approached. A quick glance at Josie and nods to Evan and Humphrey sent her children quietly out the back door.

For two years now the small homestead had been repeatedly raided. Sometimes the trespassers had been Union soldiers out from Fort Gibson on a foraging mission. Other times the intruders were Rebels attached to Stand Watie's Cherokee Mounted Rifle Patrols, who had at least thus far spared their house and barn from torches, a fate already met by many of their former neighbors. It didn't matter whether the soldiers coming down the road claimed allegiance to the United States of America or the Confederate States of America, when they left there would be little food remaining in the house for the family. If the soldiers could find anything of use or value, they would not leave it behind.

Evan and Humphrey went quickly down the grassy hillside to the small barn behind the house. Evan grabbed the burlap sack hanging on a nail just inside the door, pulled the hens from the nests where they were setting, and stuffed them into the bag. He then yanked the rooster from his perch and forced him into the sack with the hens. Their cackling and crowing ceased quickly as he tied the top, leaving them in the dark. He gently removed two fresh, still-warm eggs from the nests, placing them carefully under the shelf in the corner of the building. Then he raked his arm along the nests, scattered the straw across the floor, covered the eggs, and left no sign there had been chickens in the barn.

Meanwhile Humphrey had untied their brown-spotted milk cow and led her with her spindly-legged calf down the rocky path out the back of the barn. Evan picked up a bound broom-weed rake next to the back door and followed Humphrey, carefully sweeping away any tracks left by the boys or the cattle as they quickly made their way to the creek bed at the foot of the hill.

Josie had dashed to the springhouse where she, too, had left a burlap sack in easy reach. She pulled an earthenware bottle of milk from the cold water and placed it in the sack, adding the crock of butter stored on the small shelf in an alcove just above the water line in the side of the building. There wasn't much for her to carry this time. The soldiers were coming before the cow had been milked, and for days they hadn't had enough food for leftovers that needed a cool place for storage. Then she walked quickly down the creek bed under cover of the towering cedar trees crowding its banks. She met her brothers beneath the rocky shelf where they would wait until it was safe to return to their cabin.

Addie knew that Josie hated leaving her mother in the house with Melvina, Nicholas, and Baby D, but she told the children if the soldiers found the house empty with coals in the fireplace they would know someone had been there, and they might come looking for them. It was safer for her to stay there with the babies and convince the soldiers she was alone with her small children, left to depend on the kindness of neighbors to merely survive. Addie made up her story about which side her husband was off fighting for depending on the colors the soldiers were wearing. He was with the Union if they were wearing the faded blue coats of the soldiers from the north, but if they wore Confederate grey then he was with Watie's men somewhere in the Cherokee Nation or the bordering southern states. These stories had saved their house from the torch for two years in what was to them a senseless war. The men, women, and children living here in Indian Territory were not part of a country fighting its own Civil War.

Back in the glade next to the creek the children sat, waiting for the soldiers to leave.

"Wonder how long we'll be stuck out here this time," Humphrey said softly to no one in particular.

"I don't know," Josie answered him, "but I sure hope we won't have to be here after dark. It's getting cold now when the sun goes down."

"If you'll keep Mabel and the calf here, I'll try to sneak back up the creek to see what's going on," her brother replied. "We don't have anything for them to take, so maybe they'll just move on quickly."

"All right, but stay low and don't get caught."

Humphrey started back up the creek toward their cabin, carefully slipping into the underbrush as he rounded the first crook in the creek bed. Josie and Evan nervously watched him disappear from view. Evan turned to her and whispered, "Josie, I still don't understand why just two of us can't bring the cow and calf down here with the chickens so Mama can have one of us with her. Seems like she'd be safer with you or Humphrey up there."

"Well, Evan," his sister explained, "Mama has two things to worry about. She's afraid if Humphrey stays, and either the Union soldiers or Watie's men see him, now that he's fourteen they are liable to conscript him like they did Papa. And she says she's worried that I'm getting old enough some of those soldiers might take a liking to me, and she won't have any of that. So she sends us down here." She paused a moment. "I sure hope Humphrey's careful," and they both turned to stare anxiously at the spot where their brother had ducked under the low hanging bushes.

"Do you know when Papa will be back?" Evan asked wistfully.

"No, not this time," Josie answered. "Just whenever he can get away and find his way home safely."

Time passed slowly as they sat beneath the rocky overhang waiting for Humphrey to return. They watched a pair of fat, red-tailed squirrels chase each other along the leafy limbs of the tall oak trees at the edge of the creek, defying gravity as they jumped from branch to branch. A flock of foul-tempered crows ended the game as they flew into a nearby grove of hackberry and began fussing with each other. Far overhead a lone eagle soared in lazy circles as the sun began its slow descent toward the western hills. Finally they heard the crunch of footsteps on dry leaves as their brother came toward them then into sight, waving at them to join him.

Humphrey led Mabel, content after her afternoon of grazing along the bank of the creek, back to her spot in the barn. It was his evening chore to retrieve the milk bucket hidden among the high branches in a tree in the nearby woods and milk the cow, leaving enough to fill the belly of the calf pawing impatiently outside the stall. Humphrey skimmed the warm, foaming milk, poured it into a clean jar, sealed it tightly, then set the fresh milk on the shelf deep in the chilly water of the spring house. Finally, before returning home, he rinsed the bucket and returned it to the branch well out of sight of intruders.

Meantime, Evan had rebuilt the hens' nests, recovering the hidden eggs. Until the raiders left them alone, the hens would not be able to set on their eggs long enough to hatch another flock of chicks, so he took the eggs with him to the house to give to his mother.

Josie returned the butter to the springhouse but carried the milk she had taken to the creek back to the cabin for her mother to use that night. She hoped it had not spoiled in the warmer creek water where it had been left while they were hiding. With luck, Mama had not had to move the rug under the rocker that covered the loose board hiding their meager supply of cornmeal which was tucked away under the floor. They could at least have corncakes that night.

"I will never get used to that!" Addie fumed as her children entered the kitchen.

"Used to what?" Humphrey asked.

"These soldiers just coming in my house and prowling around. I was brought up where there was such a thing as good manners, and you never entered a house without an invitation. You certainly didn't dig around in someone else's drawers and belongings. Rude, just plain rude!"

"Did they find anything to take this time? Josie asked.

"Not really. They started to take the firewood we have left but decided there was so little it wasn't worth it. Thank goodness they didn't look in the woods where we have that pile Humphrey cut for us last week."

Checking once more to make certain the intruders were truly gone, Addie pulled the rocker aside, pushed the rug back, pried up a loose board, then lifted the sack of coarsely ground cornmeal from its hiding place. She dipped out a cupful of the grain before returning the sack to its hiding place between the floor joists under the board, then she scooted the rocker back in its place. Using one egg and just enough milk to moisten the meal, she mixed a batter that she browned in a cast iron skillet over the hot coals. The children ate the corn cake with the remaining milk for supper. It was a simple meal, but they were thankful to have at least that much. There had been nights they had climbed into bed listening to growling, empty stomachs.

CHAPTER 2

WELCOME HOME

The moon rose full and bright that evening in early October. Although it was chilly, Humphrey had banked the fire, not wasting wood for heat while they were warm under their blankets. They had all been sound asleep when Addie was awakened by a soft tapping at the front door. She rolled away from the baby nestled at her side then reached to the floor next to the bed for the strong oak pole she kept there. Rising quietly, she held the stick above her head as she tiptoed across the room, ready to strike the intruder. Then she heard a familiar voice whisper her name. "Addie?"

Her breath caught and she lowered the weapon to her side.

"Levi!" she answered as she quickly lifted the latch used to lock the door.

"Shhh! Don't wake the young'ns. Come outside. I need to talk to you before they know I'm back."

Taking only a moment to slip on a pair of Humphrey's worn boots and a jacket that were by the door, Addie followed her husband out onto the wide front porch and down the uneven wooden steps. When they reached the gate at the end of the path, they stopped under the yellowing leaves of the giant elm tree. Levi opened his arms, and Addie walked into a long awaited embrace.

It had been four weeks since the Union soldiers had taken Levi into their service at gunpoint and headed south with him, supposedly moving toward the Arkansas River near Fort Smith.

"How did you get away?" Addie asked.

"That's a long story. I'll tell all of you about that tomorrow," he promised. "We need to talk about something else first while the children aren't around to eavesdrop."

"What is it, Levi? You sound serious and that makes me nervous."

"I have bad news, and it could mean danger to all of us. I've been on the road and in hiding for days trying to get back here. You know how I feel about this war. It isn't my war, our war. But it's affecting us anyway so that's beside the point for now. I know it's been hard on you with me being gone. You have no idea how glad I am to see the house is still standing."

"Well, that's taken some creative story telling on my part here and there. Seems the soldiers want to burn everything associated with the enemy," Addie told him.

"I know. There aren't very many places between here and Fort Smith that the war hasn't touched. There are some places that have sided with Stand Watie and the Confederacy that the Union troops haven't gotten to. If anyone has shown loyalty to the North, Watie's men have burned their houses and barns, taken their livestock, and destroyed their crops. A lot of folks are almost starving to death and it ain't even winter yet." Levi shook his head sadly.

"We've heard that it is that way in Tahlequah and Park Hill, too," Addie replied. "Old man Barnes came by last week on the way down to check on his house, and he stopped long enough to share some news. According to what he said, most of the homes in Park Hill have been burned to the ground. The Union troops at Fort Gibson have taken in hundreds of the Cherokee families, but they don't have much to feed them."

Levi replied, "Andy took care of you after your folks died, and I know all of you would have been safe with him in Texas. Maybe it was a mistake not sending you with your brother when he took Annie and their children and went south with her father. I just didn't believe it would get this bad. I wanted to stay here to protect our land and home."

"I know, Levi, and I agreed with you. Don't go blaming yourself. Those who did go south are likely to come back home and find nothing is left. They'll have to start from scratch."

"Well, that brings me to what I need to tell you. We've got to get the children and get away from this house. It's too dangerous for any of us to stay here this close to the road anymore. We're too easily seen here."

"Oh, Levi, we've made it this far. We can just hide you when we hear someone coming. The children and I will be okay just doing what we've been doing."

"No, Addie. Things are changing fast. There's a guy named Quantrill up in Missouri. He's gathered up a group of soldiers who are really nothing more than a gang of outlaws, and they've started raiding surrounding states, even coming into the territories."

Levi had more information as well, news he kept to himself so he wouldn't frighten Addie more. Just a month before, in August, Quantrill's Raiders hit Lawrence, Kansas, and they massacred over 450 men and boys. They'd been coming south into Indian Territory, too. They weren't the only outlaws, either. If it were just the soldiers coming by their farm it might not be so bad, although Levi knew the soldiers been doing some pretty awful stuff as well. He was really concerned about Humphrey and even Evan being taken. Josephine might not be safe, either.

Addie sat in stunned silence. There had been little news from the outside world in weeks. Since the soldiers had taken her horses and wagon, she had been mostly isolated from her neighbors. Many of them had left anyway, seeking safety at Fort Gibson, heading south to Texas, or going west away from the fighting. She had occasionally heard the soldiers from one side or the other talk of how some skirmish had gone, or some far-away battle, but she was always doubtful of the accuracy of their stories since each side always seem to tell of their own heroics and victories, never their defeats.

She sighed and, shaking her head back and forth, she looked at her husband in despair. "Levi, where can we go now to keep the children safe and keep you from being taken again?"

"Addie, I've had some time to think about it, and I think I have a plan figured out. It won't be the most wonderful way to survive until this war is over, but I think there is a way we can do it without having to go far away. Do you think you and the children can really rough it for awhile?"

"Levi, we can do anything if it means our children will be safe. What do we need to do?"

In the waning moonlight as she rested against his chest with his arms around her, Levi told her his plans for what would become their living arrangements the next several months.

CHAPTER 3

ESCAPE

"Something sure smells good."

The thought floated through Josie's mind as she pulled herself out of a deep slumber. She rolled away from the warm body of her younger sister who was curled up in a small ball under the quilt at the edge of the soft feather bed. Josie sat up, sleepy-eyed, and crawled over five-year-old Nicholas who lay on her other side. It was then she recognized the deep voice coming through the floorboards from the kitchen downstairs.

"Papa!" Josie called, carefully sidestepping down the narrow steps to the door below. "You're home!" Levi opened his arms to his daughter as she raced into the kitchen in her flannel gown, tangled braids flying behind her.

Giving her a big hug, he then pushed her back and said, "Girl, you have growed a foot since I been gone!"

Blushing, Josie smiled at him and said, "Yes, Papa, and Mama says I'm her right hand with the little ones. We're sure glad to have you back. Are those soldiers going to leave you alone this time?"

"We'll discuss that later, after your brothers get back from their chores. I've got a lot to tell you and don't want to have to talk myself hoarse going over it all more than once," her father replied. "Meantime, how about some breakfast."

It was only then that Josie's attention turned back to her rumbling stomach and the wonderful smells that had become so scarce in their kitchen in the past weeks. She looked in the skillet resting on the coals on the hearth. "Venison?" she asked.

"Yep," Levi replied. "I got up early and went hunting. Seems there wasn't much in the cupboard around here."

Addie, smiling at her husband, said, "I told him how hard it's been keeping food with soldiers coming by every few days, claiming they needed whatever we'd managed to put together. But he's here now, and things will change for the better," Then she turned to Josie and added, "Now Girl, you get back upstairs and get dressed before the boys come back, then you can help me set the table."

Josie scrambled back up the narrow staircase into the bedroom where the little ones were sitting up in bed. "Papa's back," she said, pulling off her flannel nightgown. "Get dressed and go on downstairs. He'll want to see you." She yanked her dress over her head, pulled on her stockings, slipped her boots on her feet, and tied the laces. Then she finger-combed her hair and quickly braided it again as she descended the stairs and dashed back to the kitchen. She was ready to help with the first real breakfast they had eaten in weeks.

Once Evan and Humphrey returned from their chores, much quicker than in recent months since most of their livestock had been taken, the family sat together to share venison steaks served with corn muffins and brown gravy. Then Josie and Addie cleaned the dishes as Evan took the fat and bone scraps far into the woods. Any leftovers found around the house might tell scavengers that the family had a food supply, and that might lead to a more thorough search of their cabin. With the chores done and the kitchen clean, Levi sat down with his family to tell them his story.

September, 1863

A thunderstorm had moved through earlier that day, cooling the usually warm, early-September air. Levi had thrown extra logs on the cook stove in the kitchen to knock the chill off the cabin for the evening. A reconnaissance convoy of Union soldiers rode up to the gate just as the sun was setting. Smoke billowing from the chimney had drawn them to the homestead where the family had been gathered around the table by the fire. The chatter of the children had muffled the sound of approaching horses on the muddy road until it was too late for Levi to slip out the back door undetected.

"How come you ain't out fighting somewhere?" the captain asked him. "Watie's men leaving you alone? You a Rebel?"

"Nope," Levi had answered. "I sure ain't!"

"Well, then," the captain said, "we need you to be ridin' with us." Punching his rifle into Levi's ribs, the soldier forced him into a rickety wagon waiting along the side of the road then ordered him to take off his shoes. Three other captives, two tow-headed teenage white boys and an older Negro man, were seated on the splintered boards in the back, holding their heads in their hands as armed riders guarded them. Addie and the children stood on the porch and watched helplessly as they rode away, not knowing when or if Levi would come back to them.

The small party didn't ride far the rest of that evening, just a few miles on to the Illinois River where the soldiers made camp for the night. They tied the boys and men who been captured that day to the wagon. It would be three days before the prisoners were given food, a means of keeping them too weak to attempt escape.

It wasn't long before Levi got a sense of where the ragged bunch of soldiers was headed with their captives. They zigzagged south and east, and as they did the appearance of the homesteads improved. Watie's guerilla war raged on, and where there had been a sign of Confederate allegiance the property had been left alone. But too often they rode by smoke-scarred foundations of houses and barns, overgrown fields and gardens, and skeletal remains of livestock left in abandoned pastures. Along the way the soldiers forced two more boys, barely teens, onto the wagon, unwilling "volunteers" for their Union Army.

Late one afternoon the rag-tag group came upon a ramshackle cabin almost hidden by green briars and wild blackberry bushes that had grown up around it. The slim column of smoke rising from the collapsing chimney was the only indication that anyone still occupied the pitiful shack. Dutch, a husky soldier with a permanent frown etched on his pock-marked face, dismounted in front of the sagging front porch. Holding his long rifle to his shoulder, he kicked the door open and entered the single room of the cabin. A young Cherokee woman cowered in the corner attempting to hide two small children in the folds of her skirt. A grey-clad Confederate soldier stood in front of them with arms outstretched in a feeble effort to protect them.

"What you doin' here, boy?" Dutch demanded.

"Sir, I knowed I shouldn't have done it, but I left my regiment. I just come back here to the territory to check on my family, my wife and kids. I knowed they'd need food for winter. Just wanted to see that they'd be all right. I suppose there'll be penalty for me when I get back, but I had to come. I just had to."

But they were penalties he would never pay. Dutch pulled his rifle up to the buttons on the soldier's chest and pulled the trigger. The young man slumped to the floor as a red stain spread across the grey coat.

"This is a war," he said over his shoulder as he stalked out of the tiny room, "and he's fightin' on the wrong side. Should'a stayed in Arkansas with the rest of them damned Johnny Rebs."

Dutch pulled the door shut behind them and the party rode off, leaving the hysterical cries of the terrorized woman and her children fading behind them. Thoughts of what would happen to her and the little ones, and the horror of what he considered cold-blooded murder, haunted Levi's dreams for weeks to come.

Levi realized the meandering route they were following would soon lead them to Fort Smith located on the Arkansas River on the eastern border of the Cherokee Nation. Listening carefully to the unguarded conversations between the sergeant and his men, he learned their squad was to join a platoon that would then turn northwest. They were expecting skirmishes with Rebel troops attempting to disrupt Union supply lines. Levi wasn't interested in the skirmishes. He wasn't interested in their conflicts. He only wanted to find an opportunity to escape and find his way back to his family so he could protect them until the whole war was settled one way or another.

His opportunity came a just a few nights later. The soldiers found a deserted store on the outskirts of Van Buren to billet the squad and their prisoners for the night. It was chilly, and the soldiers built a fire in the pot-bellied stove sitting in the center aisle of the building. One of the soldiers pulled a bottle half full of corn liquor from his ragged rucksack, and it was passed from mouth to mouth as they whiled away the evening in the dark building. One by one the soldiers fell into a drunken slumber.

Quietly, the Negro scooted across the dusty floor to Levi. Although his is own hands were bound, by sitting back to back he was able to loosen the knots in the rope binding Levi's wrists. When Levi was finally able to free his hands, he quickly untied the Negro then they released the other captives from their bound wrists. They quietly raided the soldiers' rucksacks, grabbing what they could. Levi found three blue biscuits to tuck deep into his pockets. Then the freed prisoners carefully stepped over their unconscious captors and they slipped out the back door. They split up, hoping to lessen the chances of being seen before getting far away from Van Buren. Levi and the Negro man headed north through the star-lit sky, knowing they would have to sleep during the daylight hours and do most of their traveling under the cover of darkness. They would have to maneuver past both Yankee and Rebel encampments. By following the Arkansas River north to the settlement of Webbers' Falls, Levi could turn northeast there and soon be home. His companion was headed on to the northern states in search of true freedom.

They stopped at the edge of a dense woods after dashing across an open field. Levi held out his hand to the other man.

"Levi Ballew," he said.

"Nice to meet you, Massa Ballew. Don' rightly know my name, heard it was Minaw Thompson, but folks just call me Minaw," the Negro replied.

"Call me Levi. How'd you end up here?"

"Well, my Massa's family had a beautiful home in Park Hill, but it got burned up. They decided they would go to Texas, so they done loaded up and left. The Massa told me I was a freed man, even gave me a paper that said so, but they left me behind, said they didn't have 'nuf food for another mouth."

"Guess you're glad you're free," Levi responded.

"Well, I suppose so, but so far bein' free hasn't been so easy. The Rebels all think I'm a run-away, and the Yankees all think I should be fighting for 'em. I use t' have food in my belly and a warm place to sleep. Now I spend all my time hidin' and tryin' to find something to eat and a safe place to sleep."

"Sorry, Minaw. Guess this war's been tough on all of us."

Levi was well aware of the advantages of traveling after dark in the early fall. The nights were chilly, and they couldn't build a fire to keep warm, so it was just as well they kept moving in the darkness. The ticks, chiggers, and mosquitoes that would have been most annoying in the summertime were pretty much gone. A lot of the dense undergrowth had begun thinning, but there were still enough leaves to provide hiding places if they encountered unwelcome travelers. The high humidity of summertime was gone as well, and the cold of winter had yet to set in. It could have been a worse time for Levi to have to find his way home.

These were the details he told his family, leaving out the danger, hunger, and desperation he faced during his days of hiding. The stolen blue biscuits proved to be his only nourishment other than an occasional handful of nuts, dried berries, and a rabbit he speared with an long stick. In order to travel faster he and Minaw had stuck to the main trails, listening carefully for the sounds of approaching men, horses, or wagons. More than once they had to dive for cover under the deep underbrush or climb high up a post oak, thankful that the scrubby trees kept their leaves late into winter. Near Webbers' Falls they had come near a full platoon traveling in light marching order, forcing them to take cover by wading into a nearby creek and slipping behind tree roots where heavy rains had washed away the dirt. There was just enough space to hide as the soldiers, some walking along the banks and ditches, splashed through the cold water just inches from their hiding place. Levi and Minaw were chilled to the bone by the time the soldiers were finally out of sight and they could pull themselves out of the water.

Days later as they neared Fort Gibson, the men prepared to say their farewells. Minaw shared a piece of information with Levi.

"Mr. Levi, I think I sorta know 'bout where your home is. If you ever need to hide out, I know a spot you might go to. It hain't too far from you, just up from that big bend in the river east of your place. There's a big clearin' made of flat rocks, and just north of it, in the head of the holler, is a cave, or sort of a cave. I've stayed there when I been huntin' or fishin' and it got late. Lots of us Negroes knows 'bout it but not too many of you white folks do, so it ought to be safe. It ain't fancy, but it might be safer'n at your house if the soldiers are prowlin' around."

"Thanks, Minaw, that's good to know. It's something I'll keep in mind," Levi replied. He and the black man shook hands, said farewell, then parted ways.

These were the stories he kept to himself that morning as he sat in his warm kitchen surrounded by his wife and children. Whatever it had taken to get back to them had been worth it. Now he had to do what he could to keep them safe. They were going into hiding. They were going to Minaw's cave.

CHAPTER 4

MINAW'S CAVE

October 1863

The air was still as the sun rose, tinting the streaks of clouds in the eastern sky from pink to a dusky rose. Mist was rising from the stagnant water in the pools along the creek. A determined woodpecker had started his early morning search for food, the echo of his hammering drifting across the bluestem grass standing tall in the meadow behind the cabin. A thin layer of dew covering the weeds and grasses sparkled in the early morning light. Inside the cabin, every member of the family, except Baby D, was scurrying around, each intent on the chores assigned to him or her.

A flock of rusty brown and bright red cardinals lifted from the leafless lilac bush Addie had planted beside the gate in the front yard, circling into the blue sky then dipping down again as if to wave farewell. Once again Levi set out through

19

the back door with Humphrey at his side. For three days they had been loading rucksacks with whatever supplies they could carry—bedding, books, cooking equipment, and the little food they had left. They disappeared through the heavy underbrush as they slipped away from the cabin to the cave that would become their hiding place until this Civil War was over and it was safe to come home. Levi had found a smaller cave nearby, and he and Evan had taken Mabel and her calf as well as the hens and the rooster to the makeshift stable earlier that morning. Evan stayed to tend to the livestock and guard them from wildlife predators.

The hike to the shelter took over an hour. The distance wasn't so great, but it was a battle fighting the underbrush while climbing up and down the ridges along the hillside and stepping around or over stones and fallen logs. Levi unloaded his pack, then leaving Humphrey and Evan to build a fire in the rock-lined pit he had dug at the end of the shelter, he returned home for Josie, Nicholas and Melly. The children had dressed in several layers of clothing, each holding a cloth tied tightly around his or her favorite belongings. He reminded them not to follow directly behind him but to spread out so they would not leave a clear trail. For that reason he had taken a slightly different route each trip he had made to the shelter. Addie told him she would be ready to leave as soon as he returned for her and Baby D. Standing in the doorway, she waved good bye as Levi and the children were swallowed by the dense underbrush of the woods.

Levi led his children first along the rocky creek bed, but they soon left it to turn into a hollow stretching between a steep bluff and a tree covered hillside. Reaching the head of the small valley, they started the uphill climb. It wasn't a steep slope, but dodging thorn-covered blackberry vines and green briars slowed their progress. They wound around ivy covered stumps from fallen trees and through thick groves of persimmon, hackberry, and elm trees. Finally reaching a wide expanse of moss covered slate rock, Levi waited until the children joined him before they skirted the rock then slipped through a narrow crevasse and across the dry bed of a wet-weather creek. He pointed up the hillside where they saw Humphrey waving at them. Then they got their first look at their new home partially hidden behind rocks and brush.

Levi saw the shock in the children's expressions as they stared at what they expected a *cave* to be, the place where they were to live until they could return home. It was not a small opening in the side of the hill leading into a room-sized space inside the bluff, the kind of cave he knew they were expecting. Instead there was a deep gash in the hillside that was overhung with huge, flat sandstone ledges. Levi could barely stand under the front of the bluff; the rocks gradually sloped back from a height just over six feet at the front edge then dropped back into the hillside to a height of no more than eighteen inches. The gash was long, stretching down the side of the slope for nearly thirty feet.

Levi pointed out droplets, fed by underground springs, which constantly rolled over bright green moss along the front edge of the overhang before falling to the leaves below. Crocks could be placed where the drops fell, providing a source for water throughout the winter. More moss, varying in shades from white to a deep orange, coated the ceiling of their hide-away, the soft cover crumbling when touched. A deep layer of rich soil carpeted the floor where, for lack of direct sunlight, no plants grew.

The south facing would be a great advantage when the north winds blew fierce as winter approached. Levi had explained how they were going to survive. It would be a lot of work for all of them, but the children knew they could do it. They were here, and surprised or not at what they saw, they were going to help Mama and Papa make the best of this situation.

Overheated from the long walk from home, the children began to strip off the extra layers of clothing they had worn through the woods. They immediately felt not only cooler but lighter as well. Each of them took his or her little bundle of belongings and claimed a spot under the enclosed portion of the ledge where they unpacked the meager contents, folding their clothes to add to each pile.

Several large boulders had fallen along the edge of the bluff, and the boys had started piling rocks between them. In this way they were creating an enclosed space that could be heated, a space where the family could survive in some degree of comfort throughout the winter. Levi and Humphrey had already completed the arduous task of moving as many large rocks as they could find to the end of the bluff, forming a ragged wall that gave the appearance of a rock slide.

Levi left for his final trip back to the house so that he could escort Mama and Baby D to the shelter. He instructed Josie, Melly, and Evan spread out and find broken limbs that they could carry back to scatter across the rock wall. He had made it clear to them that they had to all help camouflage their hiding place and no time could be wasted.

Meantime, back at the cabin Addie knew it would be at least three hours before Levi could make his way back for her and Baby D. She had packed the final belongings they would be able to take, and now the house, her home for ten years, felt deserted. The cast iron stove stood cold and the dining table empty, the beds were stripped of linens, and the furniture Levi had made with such care for their living room seemed forsaken. Addie stepped into each of the four rooms holding Baby D against her shoulder as memories drifted through her mind.

Levi had built the cabin while they were still living in Tahlequah. He had been working as a cowhand on the Cookson ranch, but he knew he wanted a place of his own. After Addie had first refused his offer of marriage, Levi had begun laying claim to several tracts of land, gradually becoming landlord of several hundred acres. In the way of his ancestors, he could not own the lands of the Cherokee Nation for they belonged to all the People. However, he could claim it, and he would own any improvements he made on the land.

He also picked the spot for this cabin that would eventually become their home. It was near a spring-fed creek which ran year round, even in dry seasons. Tall oak and cedar trees grew around the edges of the clearing where the house would be built. The cedar would slow the winter winds, and the oak would give shade from the summer sun but let the winter sunshine warm the house. The barn, smokehouse, and other outbuildings would be built on nearby level spots. There was even a perfect garden area close by, a small fertile meadow which needed only plowing before the first vegetables could be planted.

Meantime Levi still had his courting to do. He didn't have many opportunities to ride all the way into Tahlequah, but he took every opportunity available to see the girl who had taken his heart.

Tahlequah opened its first school in 1845, and after months of study Addie was prepared to apply for a teaching position.

The school board was delighted. Here was a young lady who not only could read, write, and understand mathematics, she even knew a lot about history, geography, and other subjects they hadn't even expected to offer. She was single, a requirement for any female who planned to teach. So for two years, while Levi quietly slipped in and out of her life, Addie taught at the elementary school. Gradually she began to realize how deeply she cared for this persistent cowboy. When he finally convinced her to marry him and she accepted, she was asked to resign.

In the early years of their marriage there was no question about where they would live. Addie's father had become an alcoholic after her mother's death, and his health was steadily declining. She would not leave him, so she and Levi lived in the house her family had moved into when they first came to Tahlequah. During the week Levi continued to work as a cowhand a the Cookson Ranch, but when he wasn't working there, he spent every opportunity clearing trees, plowing the garden, or building the cabin on their own land. Addie joined him on Sundays so she could help, but their time together never seemed to be enough for the young couple. Nonetheless for awhile that was all they had.

During this time, since as a married woman she could no longer teach, Addie once again helped her brother Andy with the mercantile that their father had opened years before. Annie, her sister-in-law, had been working with him, but since the birth of their twin boys she had little time or energy to spend at the store.

Addie was grateful, although she felt a sense of guilt as well, that it was Andy who had gone to build the fire for her and Father on that fateful October afternoon. He had returned to the store with a stricken look on his face.

"Addie," he began, but she didn't need to hear his words to know what he was going to say.

"It's Father, isn't it," she had replied. "He's gone?"

"Yes," Andy answered, reaching for his sister. They embraced for a long moment, remembering the father they had known as children, the strong man who had led them from Georgia to build their home in what had been the unfamiliar Indian territory.

Andy had found Eph slumping peacefully in his chair, still and quiet, his eyes closed. Although they both felt the loss of their father, they also believed he had gone to be with his beloved Mindy where he had wanted to be since her death. The next afternoon he was buried on the hillside west of town next to his wife.

The next few years passed quickly. Humphrey was born, then Josephine, followed by Evan and Melanie. Levi had continued working for the Cookson Ranch while gradually starting his own herd of cattle and finishing their home in his spare time. She remembered clearly the day when they were finally able to load the wagon with their belongings and move to the cabin, leaving behind in that other house the sad memories of Mother, Father, and her little sister.

"Will you miss living here, being in town?" Levi had asked her.

She had answered honestly. "Yes, in many ways I will. I have friends that I won't be able to visit very often, and of course I'll miss seeing Andy, Annie and the children. It will be different, not having the store so handy when I need something. I'll have to keep a good shopping list and do a better job of thinking ahead for what we need when we do come to town. There are some good memories I'll be leaving in this house, too, as well as the sad ones. But I'm ready to move on to our own home. Let's go."

Now Addie gazed out the back door at the barn and fields, proud of all Levi had accomplished. She knew there was a possibility some of the buildings would be gone when they could finally return home. But if they could keep the children and each other safe until this war ended, the buildings wouldn't matter. She saw Levi as he came through the trees at the edge of the field and waved to him as she gathered up the last of the belongings to take with them into hiding.

CHAPTER 5

FINDING FOOD

Food was going to be a problem. The whole family became acutely aware of that by the end of November. There hadn't been much to bring with them, and in spite of the boys' hunting and fishing, there just never seemed to be enough to fill up eight bellies. Of course, Baby D didn't eat much yet, but she needed most of the little bit of extra milk that Mabel was still making, so there was that much less for the rest of them.

The children, cautioned about going too far from their shelter, had taken sacks and gathered the walnuts, hickory nuts, and pecans from under nearby trees. Evenings were often spent hulling and cracking the nuts then pulling out the meat inside. Humphrey found a persimmon tree, and they gathered the orange fruit which ripened only after frost. They all laughed at Nicholas as his mouth puckered up when he bit into a persimmon which was not yet totally orange. For a few days all of them except Nicholas enjoyed the sweet, smooth taste of the fresh fruit.

"Addie," Levi began after another skimpy lunch of beans and nuts and dried out berries, "I've got to go hunting."

"I agree," she replied. "It'd be great to have some venison if you can find a deer. But squirrel, or rabbit, or turkey would be good, too."

"No, not that kind of hunting," he said. He looked at her thoughtfully. "You mentioned that a lot of our neighbors had

27

left. Tell me about the ones who lived off the main roads who are gone. Which ones of those moved away?"

"Well, of course, but why?" she asked.

"I'm going to take the boys, and we're going scavenging. If there's anything left in their root cellars, gardens, kitchens . . . wherever, we're bringing it back here. It's not doing them any good, and if the soldiers haven't found it yet it'll only be a matter of time before they do."

"Oh, Levi, won't that be like we're stealing from them?" Addie cried.

"Now Addie, think about it. If we were in Texas or off to California and some of them were in our place, would you mind them taking what we left behind?"

She paused. "Well, no. I guess we really need to do this for the sake of the children. When our neighbors come home and we all get back on our feet, we can settle up with them then."

"Okay. Now, where should we start?"

Addie gave him names of former neighbors who had left three nearby homesteads that were far off the roads and back in the hills. The soldiers might have missed them. Levi took Humphrey and Evan, each carrying two burlap sacks, and they quickly disappeared into the woods.

The day passed slowly. Addie and the older girls tended their few chores then played tic-tac-toe and checkers with the smaller children to distract them as much as possible from their growling bellies. Addie knew one meal a day was hard on the older children, but Nicholas and Baby D just didn't understand why there was no food to eat. Addie worked on lessons with the older children, determined to continue their educations even though they couldn't attend school. The lessons served to distract them from their hunger as well. Addie was relieved and hopeful when she saw her husband and sons at the edge of the underbrush making their way up the hillside to the cave.

"Any luck?" she called anxiously.

"Some," Levi responded, and each of them held up bulging sacks.

Addie didn't even care what was in the burlap bags as long as they contained edible food. Her babies would get to eat that night, and she was very, very grateful.

"Come!" she demanded. "Tell us about your adventure."

Laughing, they brought their treasures into the cave and laid the sacks on the dirt floor.

"Don't you want to see what we brought back?" Levi asked.

"Certainly," Addie replied. "But you can talk while you unload."

"Well," Levi began, "I hate to disappoint you, but there wasn't much of an adventure. We didn't see another living soul, which is probably a good thing. The country seems absolutely deserted."

"We stopped at the Bearpaw place first," Humphrey added. "There wasn't anything left around there. It looked like either the soldiers or some other scavengers had been there."

"Where did you find what you have here?" Addie asked.

Levi answered, "Way back at the Thorne place. I never could figure why they chose that spot so far back up in the ridges, but it sure worked for us. Looked like no one had been around in months. They still had a lot of vegetables in their garden although they are pretty much dried out. We're going back to get more corn. There's still some on stalks standing in the garden. We found some useable food in the house, more beans, and some cornmeal. There was even some lye soap, and Evan found some oats out in the shed they used for a barn. They had a little bit of salt pork in their smokehouse but not much."

"Thank goodness," Addie said, the relief she felt obvious in her voice.

"We'll have food to last a while at least."

"Yes, but," Levi cautioned, "we'll have to be sparing how we use it. Right now we don't know where or when we will find much more. The boys and I can continue to hunt and fish, but with winter setting on, it won't be long before that will become really difficult."

"Right," Addie replied reluctantly. "But for now, let's get this stored inside where it can stay safe and dry. Then Josie and I will start a real dinner."

CHAPTER 6

BLIZZARD

There hadn't been any Christmas that year, at least not like Christmases past. There were no decorations, or gifts, fancy dinner, or friends stopping by. The family just sang a couple of carols, then Addie read the Christmas story from the Bible, and that was it.

January of 1864 came in quietly, then a week later winter set in with a vengeance. It was mid-morning when clouds began piling up in the northwest sky, rolling in thick with heavy dark underbellies. The first flakes of snow had been pretty, the fat and fluffy kind that cover the trees and bushes making a white winter wonderland. But soon the north wind grew stronger, becoming cold and cutting, swirling around, driving the snow parallel to the ground, and obscuring the horizon. Josie and Melly grabbed clothing and straw and began stuffing them in the cracks in the makeshift wall, cracks that were letting the wind-blown snow force its way into their shelter.

Levi came up the hill from tending the animals and pushed his way through the deer skin hanging across the opening into the shelter. "Humphrey, Evan, bundle up tight and get outside. You need to scoop up as much of that snow as you can and pack it between the rocks on the outside wall. Remember how you used to make snow forts? Do it like that. It'll help keep the wind out."

Then Levi went back outside, returning in a few minutes with an armload of wood for the fire. He stacked the broken limbs against an inside wall, then dashed back out again and returned with another load of wood. He was filling up as much space as possible with the dry tinder that had been stored at the far end of the overhang. Addie moved the bedding and clothing closer to the fire to make room for the firewood.

"We can't pack any more snow. It's turning to ice!" Humphrey called out as he pushed his way through the makeshift door.

"And it's getting slick fast," Evan added, coming in quickly behind his brother. Both were shivering and covered with snow.

"Levi, is there room for the animals up here?" Addie asked. She recalled another ice storm years ago when it was several days before her father and Andy had been able to reach their livestock.

Surprised, he answered, "Yes, but it might get a bit smelly. Then again, there'd be that much more body heat to keep this space warm." He turned to the boys and said, "Let's go get them before it gets any worse."

Levi and the boys went out into the storm again leaving Addie surveying the cave, wondering where they would find room for their animals in the rapidly decreasing space. Mabel and her calf would have to stay near the front because Mabel wouldn't be able to stand up very much farther back under the sloping roof. The chickens and rooster could just roam free. Levi wasn't concerned much about the mess they might make. He knew there would not be much food or water for them the next few days so they wouldn't be producing much manure. What they did make could be scooped up and moved as far away as possible. When it dried, it could be used as additional fuel for the fire.

Within moments Humphrey returned. He had a rope around the calf's neck and was dragging the unhappy animal through the deerskin opening. He quickly slipped off the rope and pushed it, bawling, into the cave.

"I've got to hurry back for Mabel. Evan is getting the chickens, and Papa is getting some hay. We won't be able to stay out much longer." Then he disappeared into the white curtain of snow pellets and freezing rain.

Evan came through the door next carrying a burlap sack. He opened it and dumped the chickens and rooster on the floor. The chickens quickly scurried to the back of the shelter, frightened by both the storm and the sudden removal from their familiar coop. The rooster strutted around a bit before joining the hens in the dark recesses of the cave. Josie scooped up some loose hay they were using for mattresses and crawled back to them, scattering the hay around for the little flock to serve as nests.

"I'm gonna help Papa with some hay. I'll be back with him in just a minute," Evan called over his shoulder, then once again he vanished into the storm.

Humphrey came back with Mabel who ambled through the door and went straight to her calf, mooing softly. He waved a quick good-bye and slipped out once again. Addie herded Mabel and her baby to a spot near the front of the cave that was near the fire so the ice that had fallen on their backs could melt more quickly. When Levi got back he could give them some hay.

In just a few minutes Addie heard rustling outside. The hay Levi brought over from the stable was being pushed far back into the end of the cave outside of the living space they were using. After stomping the ice from their boots, Levi and Humphrey once again pushed aside the deer skin door.

"Where's Evan?" Addie asked when she realized only two of them had returned.

"Isn't he here?" Levi responded as he started to remove his coat. "We thought he stayed with you when he brought the chickens up."

Addie's eyes widened in fear. "No. He said he was going back down to help you and Humphrey with the hay. We haven't seen him since."

Levi looked at Humphrey then at Josie. "Josie, wrap up. Be sure you get your gloves and scarf. Humphrey, get two ropes, the longest you can find. We've got to find him and find him fast."

When Addie pleaded with Levi to let her join them, he replied, "No, Addie. You stay here and fix some sassafras tea. We'll all need something to warm us inside when we get back. Please build up the fire. The little ones need tending, and they'll want you here." Then he assured her, "We'll bring him back, so don't worry."

As Josie followed Levi through the door, she realized the full force of the storm that had been hammering her father and brothers. It had turned from a snow storm into a raging blizzard. The howling wind blew the snow pellets and freezing rain parallel to the ground, and the ice was almost sharp enough to cut their skin. Within seconds their noses and ears felt frozen, and they quickly wrapped their heads and faces. Visibility was limited to no more than a few feet. How would they ever find Evan?

"Grab the end of this rope, Josie," Levi commanded. "And Humphrey, you grab the end of the other one. We're going to spread out as far as the ropes will go. Be real careful and whatever you do, don't drop your rope. If you find Evan, yank twice real hard and we'll follow your rope to you. Humphrey, you stay to the left where you can see the bluff so we can find our way back. Let's go."

Slowly they began walking down the slippery hillside, calling for Evan as they went, the wind tearing the frantic calls from their lips. It was nearly impossible to see through the thick veil of frozen white, but they protected their eyes as best they could and strained to see through the semi-darkness. It seemed forever, but it was only moments before both Humphrey and Josie felt two strong tugs on their ropes. They quickly followed the ropes back to their father.

Levi was pulling rocks away from Evan's foot, and as he quickly freed the boy's ankle he commanded, "Humphrey, lead us back your direction to the bluff. We'll follow it home. Evan, don't talk. You can tell us what happened later." He lifted the boy into his arms then followed Humphrey back along the bluff.

By the time they made their way back to the shelter Evan was shaking uncontrollably. Addie had the fire burning, and she quickly stripped his wet clothing from him then wrapped the boy in a warm blanket. As the shaking subsided to shivers, she began encouraging him to drink the hot tea.

"You need to warm up inside, too, Evan. Drink up," Levi told him. He held the cup for him as he began sipping the steaming beverage.

"All of you, too," Addie demanded of Levi, Humphrey, and Josie. They had quietly slipped off their wet coats, hats, gloves, and boots as Addie began tending to Evan. Josie found three mugs and filled each of them with the hot tea. The warmth of the liquid began radiating through their bodies from the inside as the heat from the fire warmed their skin. They sat quietly around the fire waiting for Evan to warm enough to tell them what happened. Sounds of the storm continued to rage outside, but they had closed their shelter tightly enough to keep most of the wind and cold at bay, at least for the moment.

"Mama, I hurt." Evan's voice was soft and weak.

"Where does it hurt, Son?" Addie asked.

"My ankle most of all. But I can't feel my toes or my fingers."

Addie carefully pulled the blanket away from Evan's leg and looked at his ankle. It was red and swollen, but when she gently felt it she could find no sign of broken bones. His toes, however, were more of a concern. They were still cold and white, signs that the circulation had not returned to them. She pulled his hands from under the blanket and examined his fingers as well. They, too, were white and hard, as cold to the touch as icicles.

"Girls," she nodded to Josie and Melly, "your brother needs help. Each of you take one of Evan's feet and hold it next to you and rub it. Stay away from that ankle, and be gentle. We don't want to rub any hide off. Rub down toward his toes. I'll take one hand and do the same. Levi, will you take the other?"

Levi sat next to his son and the four of them began stroking the boy's hands and feet, hoping to return the circulation so he would not lose toes or fingers to frostbite. It was going to be a long night.

"Wake up, Addie," Levi's voice penetrated Addie's sleep. Exhausted, she forced herself awake, fighting the desire to close her eyes and drop back into dreamless slumber.

"What is it?" she whispered, carefully unwrapping herself from the blanket then tucking it back around Evan. The cave was frigid, and the moaning of the wind wrapping itself around the trees and hills slipped through the door with the icy air.

Levi carefully placed a log on the fire and stirred the glowing embers. Then in the dim light he pointed to Evan's hand that had slipped from under the covers. Addie examined it carefully. Her eyes met Levi's and concern for the boy flashed between them.

"I need to get to Tahlequah," he said quietly.

"Why? What for? We need you here," Addie replied anxiously.

"We're going to need some medicine, and I'm afraid we need some liquor, some strong corn liquor," he answered.

Puzzled, Addie asked, "What for? I don't understand."

"Yes, you do. Look at those fingers, Addie. What do you think is happening to them? At least two of them aren't going to recover, and you know what I'll have to do if they get gangrene."

Tears welled up in Addie's eyes as she let herself comprehend what Levi was saying. If the fingers, and possibly some toes, had to be cut off, they needed something to give Evan to knock him completely out. Whiskey was the only thing that might possibly be available.

"Can you get there and back in time, before this gets in his blood stream?" she whispered.

"The blizzard has let up, so I think I can walk a couple of miles an hour. I can get to town by this afternoon. I think I'll be safe staying on the main road. The soldiers will be hunkered down trying to keep warm and dry, so there shouldn't be any danger from them. I'll see if any of our old friends are still around town. Maybe they can help us, then I'll start right back." He continued, "I'll be better off walking than trying to camp somewhere tonight. That way I can keep warm."

"How can you walk, Levi?" Addie challenged. "A lot of that is ice out there. You won't be able to stand up, much less walk."

"I learned something from Andy and your father a long time ago. They showed me how to make what they called snow shoes. I'll make a pair of those and I'll strap them to my boots. That'll help make walking possible," he assured her.

"Levi, I hate to ask," Addie began hesitantly, "but if you have a chance to find anything in the way of food, you know we could really use it. I'll put some more beans on the fire, but we just don't have much of anything else, and you can't possibly go hunting until this storm moves out."

Levi looked sadly around their shelter. "I know, Addie. This is a lot rougher than I thought it would be. I could just kick myself for not sending y'all to Texas with your brother, but that's water under the bridge now. I'll see what I can find."

He took a few minutes to stack some wood closer to the fire, pulled his coat on, then stepped outside to chip some ice into a bucket so they would have extra water for the cattle when it melted.

"It doesn't look like it 'cause it's so cloudy, but it's almost daybreak. I need to go so I can get back. You take care, Addie, and let Humphrey and Josie help. Mostly you just all need to stay in here and keep warm." He wrapped his arms around her for a quick farewell.

"You are the one who needs to take care, Levi. Be careful, and stick to the main road. If you aren't back by tomorrow afternoon, someone will come looking for you." She hugged him in return, then as soon as he slipped through their deerskin door she pulled it shut and tied it tight against the cold and wind. Checking to see that the children were all covered, she added a small log to the fire and began the long vigil, waiting again for Levi to return.

CHAPTER 7

SEEKING HELP

It seemed the sun never really rose that morning. The sky just gradually became lighter behind the thick layer of grey clouds that lay low against skeletal line of trees along the horizon. A few determined snowflakes were still sputtering their way to the ground, but the storm itself had passed. The woods were silent in the early morning. With the wisdom of instinct, all the furry and feathered creatures had gone to ground, staying sheltered until the worst of this storm, and the cold it brought with it, had cleared and the sun returned. Levi tromped carefully through the white silence of the timber and underbrush until he reached the two ruts that passed for a road in the backwoods area.

Time seemed to pass in slow motion as Levi fought his way in the snow-muted silence down the narrow, ice-coated roadway. Although they were bulky and somewhat awkward, he was grateful more than once for the snowshoes he had strapped to his boots. They had grabbed the ice when he had slipped, keeping him from a certain tumble. He knew he could ill afford to fall and hurt himself, because as cold as it was the only thing keeping him from freezing was constant movement.

After the first couple of hours of fighting his way up and down the hills, the road began to widen. There were more homesteads, or what remained of them, set back from the trail. Snow cover softened the burned out remains of what had been homes, barns, and outbuildings for many of the families Levi had known, families who had fled the area, seeking safety elsewhere. He hoped they had found food and shelter wherever they had gone.

Subdued lighting had reached overhead by the time Levi had crossed a rolling plateau and then, standing in a clearing where the road dropped sharply, he looked across the valley toward Park Hill. This hill was the steepest he would encounter, and the road turned abruptly downward before disappearing into the snow-laden trees. He was grateful that the ice had begun to melt just enough to form a crunchy surface that the snowshoes caught and held to more easily as he cautiously walked down the hill and into the woods.

After descending the steep hillside and following the tree line along the base of the slope, Levi continued across a wide, white meadow. Except for the crunch of his snowshoes on the icy surface, he was surrounded by silence. Soft white fog came from his lips and formed frost on his beard and moustache, and he kept his hands close to his body and under his armpits as much as he could. He occasionally reached up to pinch his cheeks and nose to keep circulation going.

Reaching the other side of the meadow, Levi spotted a large animal which he soon realized was a bay gelding. On its back were a plain saddle and loaded saddle bags; the horse's reins dangled alongside its head and hung limply to the ground. Moving restlessly, it pawed the ground and circled a snow covered pile lying near its hoofs. Coming closer, Levi realized the lump in the snow was a grey-coated Confederate soldier. He rushed as quickly as the snow shoes would allow to the man's side, but knew immediately he was much too late to be of any help. It appeared that the soldier had fallen from the horse and had frozen where he lay.

Levi thought only for a moment about what he would do. He grabbed the horse's reins and tied him to the closest tree. He pried the soldier from the frozen ground then he threw the stiff, lifeless body across the saddle. If the ground had not been frozen, Levi would have buried the soldier and taken some identification from him on to town so his family could be notified where his body had been buried. But under the circumstances, he would leave the corpse with someone to be tended to later rather than let it remain there until the wild animals found it. He led the horse the final two miles into Park Hill, hoping there would still be someone living there who could help him.

As he neared the small Cherokee settlement that had been home to so many cultural events over the past twenty years, he saw only one thin plume of smoke indicating there were still people living in the area. He didn't want to barge into a group of soldiers billeted in the two-storied house with the smoking chimney, so he tied the horse off the road behind a clump of barren blackberry vines and slipped quietly closer to the dwelling to check out the situation.

From his position at the edge of the woods Levi could see the devastation of the village. The snow and ice had blurred the outlines of the foundations where homes had once stood, beautiful homes that Levi had helped his friends build several years before. Rose Cottage, the home Chief John Ross had so lovingly built, was gone except for the four front porch pillars and the chimneys rising from each end of the ruins. Hunter Home which belonged to George Murrell was one of the few buildings still standing. Levi could only guess as to why it had not also been burned to the ground, but at that moment he was grateful to see it still standing for whatever reason.

Quietly Levi slipped up to the steps on the back porch and peered in the window. Two ladies were sitting close to a large cast iron cook stove, the source of that narrow trail of smoke. The older one turned when Levi tapped lightly on the door. Wrapping her shawl tightly around her shoulders, she shuffled to the door, opened it, and motioned him inside.

"Come in, Mister," she ordered. "You look like you're freezing."

"I am, Ma'am," he replied as he moved close to the warmth of the stove. "And I come need of some help."

"Don't know how much help we can be," she said sadly, shaking her head. "The soldiers don't respect much of anybody. They've done stole most everything we have. Name's Eliza Ross, and this here's my cousin Jane."

"My apologies, Ma'am. I should have introduced myself. I'm Levi Ballew from down south a way. My son's been hurt and has bad frostbite, and I need medicine and probably some moonshine. I fear we may have to take away some fingers and toes to save his life," he explained sorrowfully.

"Sir, we've got nothing here to help you," she told him with regret. "You best go on in to Tahlequah. They've been hit hard, too, but there might be someone left who can help. Warm up first, then you probably need to get on the road."

"Yes'm," Levi replied. "But there's something else. I found a soldier, dead and frozen, about two miles from here. Can I leave his body here and let someone take care of burial when the ground thaws? I've decided to keep the horse 'til I get back close to home and just hope none of the soldiers see me. It'd sure help me get about faster."

"Of course. Put the body in the cellar. He'd keep for a couple of days there. Not so's it matters much, but Union or Confederate?"

"Confederate grey, Ma'am," Levi replied.

Mrs. Ross handed Levi a rag to help dry the ice that was beginning to thaw on his beard. He stayed next to the stove until he felt the heat soak through his clothes and warm him.

"I can get you a cup of coffee, but it's just chicory. My apologies for not offering you food, but we just barely have enough to last for this evening's repast. We're hoping someone will stop by and leave something for us as they sometimes do."

"Oh, no Ma'am, keep the coffee for your own use, and no apologies necessary. I thank you for your fire and hospitality. It's time I move on. I can't get home 'til well after dark now depending on what I find in town. I'll just leave that young man in the cellar and be gone."

Levi, moving with more energy since he no longer felt the cold creeping into his joints, quickly returned to the horse and hauled the soldier back to the cellar behind the house. He gently lifted the frozen body, and as he laid the soldier on the floor beside the empty shelves he realized the man was really just a boy not much older than Humphrey. He shook his head at the thought of the waste of such a young life. Mounting the horse, he turned and headed down the road to cover the remaining three miles as quickly as possible. It was mid-afternoon, and he had no more time to spare. He kept an eye out for other riders, still leery of being seen by either Confederate or Union soldiers, and encouraged the horse to move toward Tahlequah as quickly as he could on the still icy road

CHAPTER 8

STORY TIME

"Mama, I'm cold, and my tummy is grumbly." Five-year-old Nicholas was the first to speak what they were all thinking.

"I know, Nicholas," Addie told him. "Come over here and snuggle up next to me. Maybe Papa will be back soon with some food. We just have to wait. I'm sorry."

The beans were long gone, divided and eaten at noon. Addie was well aware that none of the children, or herself for that matter, had gotten enough to fill an empty stomach. She was really, really hoping Levi would be able to find something to tide them over for a few more days. She was keeping the fire low, because if he wasn't back by morning the wood supply would almost be gone. Everything outside would be wet once the ice and snow began to melt, so she needed to ration what dry wood they had.

"Let's all snuggle up, and I'll tell you a story," Addie told the children, hoping to distract them. "Share your quilts; just don't get too close to the fire. Anybody have a suggestion?"

"Tell us the one about the seven sisters," Melly requested.

"Alright," Addie agreed. "Remember it is from what we know as Greek mythology. It's one of the 'Once upon a time' stories."

"I like those!" Nicholas chimed in.

"Good. Well, this is how the story goes. Once upon a time . . . ." Addie paused, "there was a mighty hunter named Orion." She stopped, knowing what would come next.

"He wasn't as mighty a hunter as Papa is!" Melly exclaimed.

"Right. He couldn't have been," Nicholas added. "I bet he couldn't shoot squirrels or rabbits like Papa does so we can have something to eat."

"You're right," Addie agreed with her children, "but the Greek thought that old Orion was a pretty good hunter. But he got himself into some trouble, so he went off to this pretty little island called Crete and became the official hunter for a goddess named Artemis. Now Artemis had these seven maids that waited on her all the time."

"Why did they wait on her?" Nicholas asked. "Couldn't she hurry up?"

Addie smiled. "No, Baby, this kind of waiting meant they helped her with her clothes, kept her room clean, combed her hair, things like that."

"Well, that's just silly!" the little boy exclaimed.

"What were their names?" Josie interrupted. She was quite familiar with her mother's version of the story.

"Well, there was Josephine, Melvinia, Desdemona, Addie, Armindia, Annie, and . . ." Here she stopped, always waiting for a seventh name.

"How about Mary?" Josie suggested. She was still fond of the older woman who had been a friend of her grandmother. Addie had told her stories of the quilting bee they joined their first year in Tahlequah, and how the group made Mary a quilt for her wedding.

"Ok, then Mary it is!" Addie agreed. "These seven maids were sisters, and they were all quite beautiful. Orion didn't have a whole lot of sense sometimes, and he fell in love not with just one of these sisters, but with all seven of them. He started following them around, and since he was such a good hunter and tracker, they couldn't get away from him."

A soft voice came from under the blanket where Evan lay. "That sounds like Papa when he's tracking a deer. It may take awhile, but he'll find it sooner or later."

"Yes, but these girls didn't like being followed, and they didn't like Orion either, at all. Finally, one of the gods took pity on them and turned them into beautiful white doves so they could fly away. Eventually all seven of them flew so far into the sky that they became stars and are still together in the heavens."

"Is that the end of the story, Mama? Didn't they live happily ever after?" Melly asked.

"Well, not quite. You see, Artemis got mad at Orion and killed him, but then she felt really bad about it, so she placed him in the sky, too. So if you know your constellations, you can find him in the nighttime sky, still chasing the Pleiades, which is what the seven sisters are called."

"Humph!" Josie exclaimed. "That just isn't fair."

"Dear, you must remember this is a 'Once upon a time' and is not a true story. The Greek, along with the Cherokee and many other people made up stories to explain how the stars, moon, and even the sun got into the heavens. Just because they tell the stories doesn't make them true," Addie reminded her.

"Of course," Josie said. "I just get carried away with the idea."

"How about a nap now for everyone," Addie suggested. "I know you don't usually sleep this time of the afternoon, but it's too cold to do anything else, and it will help the time pass until Papa comes back. Snuggle down, and I'll put some wood on the fire. Let's all think about Papa coming home quickly and safely."

CHAPTER 9

TAHLEQUAH FRIENDS

Levi paused at the top of the hill south of Tahlequah, overlooking the small village, or what remained of it. There were a few trails of smoke reaching skyward, smoke that meant there were still people living in town. Seeing no sign of a military presence anywhere, Levi urged the gelding to make its way slowly over the icy ruts that wound their way down the hillside into town.

There was no activity along the well-worn grooves that led to the main street. Levi shook his head sadly when he came to the one-acre square where once the government buildings for the Cherokee Nation stood. All were gone, burned to the ground, except for the Supreme Court Building. Stand Watie unleashed his fury with fire at those who openly supported the Union instead of the Confederacy.

Riding to the north end of the street, Levi looked for the remains of Addie's family home and business. Addie's brother Andy and his friends had built Humphrey's Mercantile during the time her father had returned to Georgia for merchandise for their store. Now only the foundation and the porch that Andy had insisted be made from the large, flat sandstones in the area remained as a reminder of where the store once stood. The small cabin where the family had lived was nothing but a pile of ashes.

Reining in the bay, Levi looked around in dismay. He had hoped to find more people here in town, people who might have supplies of food, medicine, and whiskey he could plead for. Begging was not his style, but his word was good, and he knew that if he promised to repay whatever he borrowed his friends and former neighbors would trust him to keep that promise. Thinking for a minute or two, he turned the horse onto a side road that led up a sloping hill away from the devastated town square.

Even though they had moved to their farm several years earlier, Levi and Addie still had friends in town. He hoped to find some of them who hadn't fled the area. Since the home of the Glory family was away from the center of the small town, it might still be standing. Aelie Glory would be the most likely one to still be around.

A short distance up the hill a small log house sat back from the road. It was almost hidden by a yard full of post oak, sumac, and undergrowth. A narrow, snow covered path, undisturbed by other footprints, led from the road to a large flat rock that served as a small porch. Levi dismounted, tied the horse behind the shrubs where it would be out of sight from the road, and walked carefully up the path to the rough-hewn front door.

"Aelie?" he called softly as he tapped on the door. "Aelie Glory, are you still here? It's Levi Ballew."

Levi heard rustling sounds from the other side of the door, then it swung back slowly.

"*O-si-yo*, Levi, is that really you? Come in! Come in!"

Standing before him was a petite Cherokee woman, one of the most beautiful he had ever known. At twenty-two, Aelie was only three years older than his nephews Jackson and William, but she looked younger than the boys. Her dark hair hung in a single braid down her back, and her milk chocolate skin was smooth and free of wrinkles. It always took strangers a moment to notice, first by the somewhat odd tilt of her head then the blankness in her ebony eyes, that Aelie was blind, the result of a outbreak of measles that had swept through the community when she was just an infant. Addie's family knew the full cost of that epidemic.

"Yes, Aelie. I had hoped you would still be here. It seems 'most everyone else we knew is gone."

"Many people have gone to seek shelter and safety elsewhere. I chose to stay where I know my way around," she replied. Then she smiled. "I had never taken advantage of my blindness, but that has changed. It is not just for me but for my family as well. You see, when the soldiers come and see I am blind, they move on to the next house. They have too much sympathy, at least so far, to prey on a poor blind woman, and they seem to think I am too young to be responsible for very much," she explained. "In this way I have been able to be the storehouse for all my older brothers and sisters and their families. We don't have much; there is not much to be had now. But at least we have some food and supplies."

"Oh, Aelie, then I feel bad about having to ask what I came for," Levi said sadly.

"What is it you need, Levi?" Aelie asked. "You know my family would do anything for you and your family. Addie lost so much because of us, more than we can ever repay her."

"No, Aelie, you know that is not how she feels," Levi answered firmly. "Addie knew Mindy would never want her family to point the finger of blame at you or your parents for what happened to her and Desi. Your father certainly did not mean harm when he asked Mindy to help when all of you were so sick."

"Blame or not, we will always be indebted. Addie lost her mother and sister because her mother helped us when we had the measles. Now what do you need? What can I help you with?" she asked.

Levi explained the circumstances that brought him to town in search of food and medicine. Then he asked the young woman, "Tell me about your family. Let me know what has happened to our friends here so I can take the news back to Addie."

"Levi, it hasn't been good. This war in the states has torn my family apart. Two of my brothers first joined John Drew's 1st Regiment of the Cherokee Mounted Rifles. But they went along with most of the other Cherokee and deserted right before the Battle of Bird Creek because they felt the Confederates were being unfair in the pursuit of Chief Opothleyoholo. They took their families and joined the Creek chief and fought with him against the Confederates. They were forced into the refugee camps in Kansas, and we haven't heard anything from them in months. There was an outbreak of cholera there that killed many people. We fear they may have been among those," Aelie concluded sadly.

Then she continued. "One of my sisters' sons was coming home from the store when a group of Watie's soldiers surrounded him and just demanded that he go with them. He hollered to a neighbor to tell his folks what happened. The next time they heard about him was when they got the report he'd been killed at the Battle of Elkhorn Tavern over in Arkansas." She paused for a moment before going on.

"My youngest sister and her husband left for Texas. They are living near Anne and Andy, but living conditions aren't good there, either. There just isn't enough food at any of the refugee camps, and in a lot of places in Texas the Cherokee aren't welcome.

"Three of the seven of us are gone from here. My oldest brothers still live nearby since they were considered by both sides to be too old to fight. Since my nephew was killed my sister never leaves her house and tries to keep the other two boys inside with her as much as possible. It's a sad situation," she finished.

"Aelie, I am so sorry for your family. Is it like that with all our other friends as well?" Levi asked?

"Yes," she told him. "Remember the other boys who helped you and Andy build the mercantile building?"

"Of course," Levi assured her.

"Well, Edmund and George are off fighting for the Union, Gaines is somewhere with the 1st Regiment, and last we heard Albert went west to get away from the war. Their families are gone from here as well, I think to Fort Gibson."

"Addie will be sad to hear all this news," Levi told her.

"Yes, but she will be glad to have a little food and some medicine for Evan," Aelie replied. "And we need to get to that so you can get home. How much can you carry, Levi?"

"Oh, I forgot to tell you. I have a horse." He then explained how he came into at least temporary possession of a mount that would help him carry some supplies back home. "There's a saddlebag on him, too, and I haven't checked to see what's in it. I need to look in case there is anything we can use. I hope there aren't any military dispatches, because they'll soon come looking for him if there are."

"You go get the saddlebags while I rustle you up some food and supplies," Aelie told him. "This will take a few minutes."

Levi pulled his coat around him and stepped back out into the cold, the frigid air biting his cheeks and ears once more. He returned to the horse which was restlessly pawing at the snow where it had been tied.

"Take it easy, old boy," he told the gelding. "I'll try to find you some food, too, just as soon as I can." Then he pulled the surprisingly heavy saddlebags from the animal's back and headed back to the cabin.

He slipped back in the front door and called, "Aelie, where are you?"

A muffled voice called from almost directly below him. "Here, Levi. Look over by the bed."

Confused, Levi did as he was told and saw that the small bed had been pulled away from the wall, exposing a trap door with a narrow staircase leading to a cellar underneath the floor of the room. He called down, "Can I help you?" to which Aelie replied, "No, thank you. I put things here, and I know where they are. I'll be upstairs in a moment."

While waiting for Aelie to reappear Levi placed the saddlebags on the table and began emptying them. He was delighted with what he found. On one side was a small slab of salt pork, a bag of brown beans, a parcel of coffee beans, and a packet of sugar. Stuck in among them was what seemed to be a pair of home knitted wool socks and a woolen cap. In the other side he discovered a small sack of flour, another of peanuts, two tins of meat, and even a small pouch containing tobacco. He also discovered, to his dismay, an envelope addressed to Col. William Phillips at Fort Gibson. The young soldier had been a courier, so it was likely that at any time someone would come looking for him and his horse and the message they carried. Levi had to hurry. But he felt one more container at the very bottom of the bag and was pleased to find a small package of oats, tightly tied to keep the grains from spilling.

Aelie came back up the steep staircase carrying several small packages. Levi hurried to her side to help with the bundles. As he placed them on the table Aelie dropped the trap door back over the hole and slid the bed back in place.

"That serves us well. My family finds food where they can, and my brothers get provisions from Fort Gibson and bring them here. Nobody expects a blind woman to have a hiding place, so they have been undisturbed so far," she smiled impishly. "Now let me tell you what I have for you. It's not much, but it might help."

Levi interrupted her briefly to tell what he'd found in the saddlebags, then she continued. "I don't have much in my medicine basket, but I can send these things for you. Addie is certain to know how to use them, but let me tell you to be sure. This is goldenseal. Use it to cleanse the fingers and toes before you have to cut them. If gangrene sets in, make a poultice with this wild indigo. And this is tsiyu. Use it in a tea for fever. If you run out of this find a tulip tree and boil some of its bark. It will be bitter, but encourage Evan to drink it anyway."

"Thank you, Aelie, this will be of great help to Addie," Levi told her.

"But I'm not finished. I have a bag of rice, another of beans, and a package of dried apples. There is a container of cornmeal as well. Unfortunately it has some bugs in it, but if you are willing to pick them out then it can be used."

"Trust me, it will be used!" Levi exclaimed. "We are too much in need of food to be picky."

"Pack these and leave," Aelie ordered. "On your way out of town, go by the old blacksmith shop and livery stable. Mr. Fishinghawk's son is still there, and he often has moonshine that he's made hidden around somewhere. Addie's father was a friend of Mr. Fishinghawk, and I'm sure he'll be glad to help you. But you need to go. Now."

"Yes, I know. But one other question. What do you know about William and Mary Christie?"

"They are safe. Well," she paused, "mostly so. William and their oldest son both signed on with Watie's 2nd Regiment. At the battle at Elkhorn Tavern William took a bullet to the leg and ended up losing it below the knee, and the boy lost both sight and hearing on his left side. So they are back here, just trying to hang on like most of us who haven't left."

"Thank you, Aelie. Both Addie and Josie would want to know that. I'm off now," and he gently took her small hand in both of his, pressed it softly, then tossed the loaded saddlebags across his shoulder and slipped out the door.

"Wait!" Aelie called. "Tell me where you are staying. Andy might come back and want to know."

Levi gave her brief directions to the cave from their homestead while he fed some of the oats to the waiting horse, then with a final farewell to Aelie, he mounted the animal and followed his tracks back toward town. After a quick stop at the dilapidated blacksmith shop and livery stable where Jessie Fishinghawk did give him a small crock of moonshine, Levi turned the big bay toward the setting sun and headed back to his family.

CHAPTER 10

FOREVER BOY

The night had seemed endless. Naps in the afternoon had helped pass the time, but then when regular bedtime came no one was sleepy. Addie and Josie told stories to the younger children. Then Josie helped Melly review her addition and subtraction facts while Addie helped Nicholas practice printing the alphabet. Baby D toddled around the shelter petting the cow, chasing the chickens, then playing with her rag doll. Humphrey paced around the small space, occasionally putting another limb on the fire to keep the coals hot. The fever had begun seeping through Evan's body and sapping his energy, and he lay listless next to the fire while watching his brothers and sisters. All of them were aware of the rumbling in their stomachs. When they did finally doze off, their sleep was restless, and all of them tossed and turned under the piles of blankets.

Addie would not let her children starve. The chickens stirred in their skimpy straw nests at the rear of the cave and Mabel lowed quietly to her calf in the corner near the front of the shelter. Addie didn't want to use their livestock for food because once they were gone their food supply for the future would be gone, too. No more eggs and milk, no more little chicks or calves. But that wouldn't matter if they died from starvation. Levi had until morning to return, and if he wasn't back by then, one of the chickens would become soup.

In the wee hours of the morning Addie woke from the chill in the cave and rose to put more wood on the fire. She heard the sound of a horse approaching and hoped the smoke from the fire, drifting out the front of the cave, had not given away their hiding place. She stiffened in apprehension as someone quietly pulled back the deer skin door, then realized that someone was Levi. She couldn't keep the tears from her eyes as she reached out her arms to welcome him back.

"I bring news, Addie," he told her. "But more important, I have medicine and food."

"If you'll tell me what you have, I'll start cooking now. The children are all so hungry they can't sleep well. It will be daylight soon, won't it? We can deal with Evan then," she replied. "I thought I heard a horse. Where did that come from?" she asked him.

Levi pulled the saddle bag from his shoulder and unloaded its contents as he began telling her the story of the frozen rider.

"Now I don't know what to do with that animal," Levi said. "If I turn him loose I'm afraid he'll starve or get eaten by some of the wild creatures that roam around here. But if I keep him, he might be spotted by a scouting party and give our hiding place away. That would put the children in danger. Besides, we have nothing to feed him."

"We'll keep him for now, Levi," Addie told him. "You can tie him up way back in the stable. I don't know what we can feed him, but with a horse you can go farther to scavenge for food supplies. I don't relish the idea of starving to death before this war is over!"

Levi looked at his children in the dim lighting in the cave. All he could see were their faces peeking out from under the blankets piled on top of them to keep them warm. Those faces, once full and rosy-cheeked, had become gaunt and pale. He knew the bodies under those quilts had also become thin in the past few weeks, much thinner than they should be.

He suddenly felt his mind fill with rage and he fought against it. He was so angry at this war and those who had brought it to his country. Those same people had told Levi's people they were not suitable, not desirable enough to be part of *their* society and had taken everything from his Cherokee family and friends and moved them, often by force, from their homes. They were told this would be their new country and they could run it themselves, which they had been successfully doing. Then this Civil War between the United States began, and those same people suddenly decided they wanted this land to be a part of their war, wanted the Indians to be warriors for one side or another. Why couldn't they just leave the Cherokee alone?

Levi thought about the legend of the Two Wolves that was passed down by the Cherokee. An old Cherokee told his grandson about two great wolves fighting a battle that goes on inside all people. One wolf is the black wolf; Evil is its name. It is anger, envy, jealousy, sorrow, regret, greed, arrogance, self-pity, resentment, inferiority, lies, false pride, superiority, and ego. The other is the white wolf; Good is its name. It is joy, peace, love, hope, serenity, humility, kindness, benevolence, generosity, empathy, truth, compassion, and faith. When the boy asks the old man which wolf wins, he replied simply, "The one you feed."

Levi knew he had to continue feeding the white wolf even when it was a struggle.

He didn't expect Addie to understand, even though he knew she sympathized with him. Her family had come here by choice. They had not come over that long trail where so many of his family had become ill and where his grandmother had died. It was, among other things, so humiliating. For the sake of Addie and their children he once again reigned in his anger and turned his energy into caring for his family. He could do nothing about the war, but he could try to protect them from it.

Rays from the rising sun soon began warming the morning air. The cold front proved to be short lived, and the ice and snow began melting, dripping from the trees and bushes and turning the ground into mud. Addie had prepared a welcomed breakfast of wild rice seasoned with salt pork. After they all finished eating, she instructed Josie to dress Melly and Nicholas warmly so Humphrey could take them with him when he returned Mabel and her calf as well as the chickens and rooster to their stable. She didn't want them in the cave while they tended to Evan's frostbitten fingers and toes.

"Drink this," Levi told his son, handing him a glass of clear white liquid.

"What is it?" Evan asked.

"Moonshine. Don't expect it to taste good, but after the first drink or two you won't really taste it anyway," his father replied.

"Why do I need it?"

"Son," Levi answered hesitantly, "your fingers and little toes froze, and now they are getting infected. It's called gangrene, and it's a really bad thing. We are going to have to cut them off, or the infection will go on into your arms and legs and most likely kill you. It'll hurt bad, and this liquor'll knock the edge off the pain."

"I don't want you to do that, Papa!" Evan pleaded.

"I know, son," Levi replied, "but we have to. We love you too much to lose you. Your mama has some medicine she'll give you after to help you get better, but it's going to be a tough couple of days. After that, you'll start getting well. So drink up, all you can. But," he added emphatically, "after this I don't want you ever touching moonshine again. It can really cause problems if you get to liking it."

Evan began drinking the white lightning, shuddering as the clear liquid burned down his throat. Addie and Josie started water boiling for the rags they would need clean for the amputation. Levi slipped out and away from the cave so that Evan wouldn't hear him as he sharpened his hunting knife. Finally the boy passed out in a drunken stupor, and the operation proceeded.

Tears poured down Addie's cheeks as she firmly held first Evan's right hand then each foot firmly against a flat rock so that two fingers then his little toes could be removed. Josie cringed at the procedure, but she kept clean rags close at hand to wipe the blood then wrap the wounds. It took only minutes to perform an act that would both save and change Evan's life.

Once the operation was finished the other children were called back inside. Baby D, who had curled up in her blanket during the surgery fiercely sucking her thumb, toddled over to kiss Evan's cheek. Then she placed her doll under his arm and next to his heart before she sat down next to her sleeping brother.

"Poor Evan," she said.

"You're right, baby," Levi echoed, "poor Evan."

Chilly air greeted Levi as he and Humphrey slipped through the deerskin covering the opening of their shelter. Now that the storm had passed, Levi was hoping the wildlife would be coming out to find food and water, so they were going hunting. Josie and Melly would take over the chores of feeding the livestock and finding more wood to bring to the cave to dry out.

Evan and Baby D stayed with Addie who was carefully cleansing the wound on Evan's foot as Baby D doctored her doll nearby.

"Mama?" Evan said softly from under his pile of blankets.

"Yes, son, what do you need?" Addie replied.

"Do I have to grow up? I just want to have things back like they were when I was little, when we had a house and didn't have to worry about Papa being taken away. It was better when we weren't all hungry or worried all the time. Or hurt," he added, glancing at his bandaged hand and the damaged foot sticking out from under the covers.

Addie replied quietly, "Yes, Evan, be thankful you have the chance to grow up. None of us stays young, but we all have the same feeling you have at one time or another in our lives. Would you like for me to tell you a story?"

"Yes!" Evan quickly answered. Hearing that their mother was going to tell a story, Baby D picked up her doll by its arm and dragged it to her brother's side. She carefully snuggled under the blanket next to Evan with her doll between them. The children always enjoyed their mother's tales.

"This one is about the 'Forever Boy' and the Little People."

"Oh, it must be a Cherokee legend then if it's about the Little People."

"Yes, Evan, it is. Once upon a time (always a wonderful way to start a story) there was a little boy who didn't want to grow up. He wasn't shy about telling people he wanted to stay forever a boy. Soon he even began calling himself Forever Boy. Whenever his friends started talking about what they would do and what they would be when they became full grown braves, he wandered away to play in the woods with his animal friends.

"Well, it finally came to the point where the boy's father couldn't stand it anymore. He told the boy, 'I won't call you Forever Boy again.' Then the father told the child that since he didn't seem to be able to convince the boy to grow up, the next day the child would be sent to his stern uncle who would teach him how to take responsibility for himself and stop playing all the time.

"Forever Boy was broken hearted and ran away to hide in the deep shadows of the woods. He could not stand the thought of growing up. He wandered to the river where he sat high above the rushing water and cried. He cried so hard that at first he did not see or hear his animal friends gather around him, trying to make him feel better. They were trying to tell him something in the low murmur of their animal voices, and finally he understood that they wanted him to come back the next morning, very early, to this same spot. So, dragging his feet, he made his way back to his home.

"Forever Boy tossed and turned all night and finally climbed out of his bed in the early morning hours to slip away from his father's house. As the sun began its slow ascent in the east, he sat again crying on the bluff overlooking the river, watching the water rush by before disappearing around a far away bend. He was so sad, thinking about telling his animal friends goodbye forever. But they gathered around him, talking their animal languages, and he finally understood that they wanted him to turn around.

"When he looked behind him, all the Little People were gathered at the edge of the woods, smiling and laughing. Some were white, some were black, and some were golden like the Cherokee. Many had their long hair pulled back in tails or braids. They ran forward to hug him. Then the one who seemed to be the leader told him, 'Forever Boy, you don't have to grow up. Come stay with us and be one of us forever and you can stay young. We will ask the Creator to send a vision to your parents letting them know you are alright and that you are doing what you were destined to do.' Forever Boy thought for only a moment before he decided that this is what he needed to do and he went with the Little People.

"So if you are out in the woods and think you see something, but when you look closely it isn't what you thought it was, or if you are fishing and you feel a tug at the end of your line and think it is the biggest fish ever, but when you pull it in it's a stick tangled on the end of your hook, well, that's Forever Boy. He's playing a trick on you so you will laugh and stay young in your heart."

Addie smiled at her son. "And that, dear boy, is what you have to do. Grow up, become responsible, but stay young in your heart so you can enjoy your life." She then turned to Baby D and, tweaking her nose said, "And that goes for you, too, Little One."

CHAPTER 11

MEDICINE WOMEN of the CHEROKEE

February cold seeped in every crack and crevice of the shelter, and the idea of separate beds had long gone by the wayside. All of the blankets were piled as close to the fire as was safe, and the children piled under them not only at night but during the day when they had no chores or studies to tend to. Addie and Levi slept on the side closest to the door with Baby D and Nicholas between them. Daylight hours centered around two things: food and firewood.

"Mama?"

"Yes, Josie?" Addie replied.

"What are we going to call Baby D? She's gettin' to be too old to be called 'Baby' anymore," Josie said.

"Well, I don't rightly know," Addie answered. "Desdemona is a bit of a mouthful for a little one. We could call her Desi, but that makes me think of my little sister who died. And that makes me sad, so I don't want to do that."

"Her middle name is Susanna, but that seems too big for her, too, since she's so tiny. Do you think she'd like to be called Sue?"

"Baby D," Addie said as the little girl snuggled onto her lap under the blanket, "since you aren't a baby anymore, Josie and I think you need a grown-up name. What do you think of Sue?"

A plump, red thumb found its way into her rosebud mouth as the child pondered the question. Then she yanked it out and looked at her mother then her sister.

"Susie. I'm Susie."

Josie and Addie laughed.

"Well," Addie addressed her daughters, "if your Papa agrees, that problem was easily solved. Susie," she smiled at the child, "you may go back to your dolls while Josie gets her coat and hat. We will soon be needing more firewood, and I don't want to use what is in here if there is dry wood outside."

With that, Josie tugged on her tattered coat and hat, pulled on some mittens, then slid out behind the deer hide door to go on her daily search for limbs and brush. She knew as soon as Melly finished letting the hens and rooster out of their pens to scratch around in their daily search for stray seeds and bugs, her sister would join her. Moving around outside, as cold as it was, was better than being cooped up in the smoky darkness of the cave all day.

Josie brought an armload of broken limbs that had fallen from nearby trees back to the shelter just as Melly got there. The girls wandered off down the hillside in search of more limbs that could be used for firewood.

65

"How much longer do you think we are going to have to stay here?" Melly asked her older sister.

"I don't know, Melly," Josie replied, "but I hope we can leave soon. I think I'd just as soon face those soldiers as live in that cave much longer."

"Well, yes, but I sure wouldn't want them to take Papa again, or Humphrey. It just doesn't seem like there's any place safe in the world anymore," she said sadly.

Josie sat down on a tree stump, resting in the warm sunshine. Her shoulders were slumped as she gazed through the leafless trees down to the river. Sighing, she turned to her little sister.

"You're right, Melly. I don't think there is a safe place, either. But Papa and Mama are doing the best they can for us. At least we are here, away from the main road where the soldiers came through all the time. Probably everybody is hungry and cold this winter, at least from what Papa said Aelie told him. So we just have to hang on and try to help as much as possible, and maybe sometime soon we can go back to our house, and our beds, and our old lives. Won't that be just wonderful?"

Melly grinned. "Yes, that sounds great. I can hardly wait."

Josie then motioned to her and they began picking up another load of limbs to haul back up the hill to keep them warm, at least for the moment. Josie remember hearing that gathering wood warms you twice, once as you gather it then again when you burn it. She knew that was really true.

They entered the cave as Addie finished wrapping Evan's healing foot and hand. He could hobble around the shelter and was learning to use a hand with two fingers and a thumb. Part of each day he spent trying to work with a bow and arrow, getting his balance and aim back so he could eventually go hunting again.

Melly watched her mother's swift, efficient movements before asking her,

"Mother, how do you know so much about medicines and treatments, how to make sick people feel better?"

"Aelie's mother taught me," Addie replied. "After my mother died and everyone was well again, Mrs. Glory asked me to come see her. She told me she wanted to help me learn those things my mother had not had time to teach me, and her medicine wisdom was one of those things."

Addie turned to her girls. "I need to be teaching you as well, my daughters. You should have a knack for it because you are of the Wolf Clan."

"What does that have to do with it?" Josie asked.

"Well, according to Cherokee legend, the women of the Wolf Clan are known as the medicine women of the Cherokee," her mother replied.

"What legend?" Melly asked.

"Are you ready for another story?" Addie replied with a smile.

"Of course!" the girls responded in unison.

And their mother began, "Once upon a time an old man, sick and covered with horrible sores, came out of the forest and into the land of the Cherokee. He came to the first clan, perhaps the Deer Clan, and asked an old woman, 'Can you help me? I am ill.'

"The old woman looked at him and said in disgust, 'We can't help you. Go away!'

"So the old man moved on to another clan, perhaps the Blue or Bear Clan, and asked an old woman, 'Can you help me? I am ill.'

"The old woman looked at him and said, 'We have children here. We don't want you to make them sick. Go away and leave us alone.'

"So the man traveled on the to the Wolf Clan. Again he asked an old woman, 'Can you help me? I am ill.'

"The woman looked at him and said, 'Go into our house and lie down on the bed. We will do everything we can to help you become better.'

"The old man did as he was told, then he instructed the woman to go into the woods and get some bark from a wild cherry tree to boil. She did as he instructed, then he took a large drink of the cherry water. Before many sunsets he was well again.

"During this same time he told the woman to go back into the woods and bring back the bark from a willow tree and make it into a poultice. Again she did as she was told, beating the willow bark between two rocks until it became soft. He placed the willow bark poultice over his sores and soon they were gone.

"After the old man was healed, he got out of his bed. Over and over again he sent the women of the Wolf Clan into the forest, telling them every time the cure for a certain ailment.

"Then one day he turned to the women of the Wolf Clan and told them, 'You have been good to me and helped me become healthy again. I have taught you all the cures that can be found in the forest. From this time on you shall be known as the medicine women of the Cherokee. When anyone becomes ill or injured, they shall turn to you and with all the knowledge of medicine you possess you will help them become well again. You are all blessed, women of the Wolf Clan.'

"Then he turned and went back into the forest from which he had come, never to be seen again."

Josie and Melly smiled at each other.

"Then we are medicine women?" Melly asked.

"Only if you are willing to learn what you can about what I learned from Mrs. Glory, and maybe someday Aelie can help you learn even more," her mother replied. "And Susie, too," she finished, looking down at her youngest daughter with a smile.

That evening they added another lesson to their daily routine: medicine.

CHAPTER 12

UNINVITED GUEST

One afternoon in late February, Addie spread a patchwork quilt across some dried grass in the warm winter sun. It was piled with several worn shirts and dresses, clothes that Levi had found in an abandoned house when he had gone foraging the week before. The dirty old clothing had been washed and dried. Addie left Josie and Melly to their chore of carefully pulling the threads from hems and seams, taking the material apart so it could be reassembled into something someone in the family could wear.

"I'm bored," Josie said.

"Me, too," Melly echoed.

"I thought when Papa said we would be living in a cave that it would be fun, kind of like going on a long picnic," Melly whined, "but this hasn't been fun. It's been work and cold and I am so hungry!"

"I know. Me, too," Josie agreed.

Even in hiding Addie had kept them all on a routine. Levi would get up early and add wood to the fire to knock off the worst of the cold, but it was still chilly in their shelter. They slept in their clothes to help keep warm, the girls snuggled together on one mound of dried grass which covered by quilts, while the boys stretched out on another pile. The grass quickly became damp from the moisture in the shaded overhang, so the boys took turns hauling it outside on sunny days to spread across the rocks to dry. The girls in turn shook out their worn blankets and spread them across a large dry boulder just at the edge of the overhang.

Addie always tried to have something for breakfast, but sometimes there wasn't much to be had. Mabel was barely giving enough milk for the calf, and the chickens no longer laid eggs in the cold weather. Food supplies had grown scarcer and scarcer.

Levi had rousted Humphrey early that morning.

"Humphrey, rise and shine," he had whispered, poking him in the ribs. "We are going hunting today and we will absolutely not come back empty handed."

Evan watched with sad eyes. "Papa," he said, "I'll practice while you're gone. I'm getting better every day. My feet are healing fast, so maybe next time I can go with you."

Humphrey crawled out from under his blanket shaking the hay from his hair and sleep from his eyes. He found his bows and quivers of arrows, knowing this would be a silent hunt, no sounds from gunshots allowed. Any noise that carried might be heard by the Union troops, now firmly in control of Fort Gibson, who regularly canvassed the area, or by Watie's rebel guerrillas who seemed to be always on the move.

In the past few days it seemed that a column of smoke arose continually somewhere in the distance. Levi had gone scouting and had come back with unsettling news. The Union commander at Fort Gibson, Colonel Phillips, had turned his troops south with orders to burn everything in their path. Dried fields and pastures, homes, and any other buildings still standing were set ablaze. The U. S. Federal government intended for those left in Indian Territory to know who was in charge, discouraging cooperation with any of Stand Watie's forces. Anyone who was armed and who opposed them was shot on the spot, leaving the bodies on the ground as the troops made their way south, intent on reaching the Texas border.

"Papa, can't we go hunting with you?" Melly had begged as Humphrey joined him with his bow and arrows clutched tightly in his hands.

"No, Melly, you don't know how to shoot, and Mama needs you here. The fewer of us out making a disturbance the better. But," he added with a smile, "I promise to take you and Josie fishing in a couple of days. How does that sound?

Melly sighed, then said, "That will be fine, Papa, just so long as we finally have something interesting to do."

Levi and Humphrey slipped quietly away, disappearing around of the rocks piled at the side of the cave that blocked the view inside. Now Melly and Josie sat outside with the pile of clothing in their laps, bored, but grateful the sun was shining warmly on that day.

Josie stopped the unraveling of the tattered shirt in her lap, tilting her head to one side. "Shush," she whispered to Melly as she began scooping up the pile of rags. "Someone's out there. You get all this inside while I slip down to put Mabel in her shelter. Tell Mama where I've gone and help her with Susie."

Melly grabbed the old clothing, piling it in the blanket before pulling the ends together to make a quick carry-all. She slipped inside the entrance to the cave as Josie cautiously made her way down the hillside, careful to not step on any rocks that might slide and create a disturbance. When she reached the tree where Mabel was tethered, she loosened the rope and led the docile cow behind the rocks with the calf following closely behind. To make certain the cow didn't moo in protest, she threw a few handfuls of the precious hay in the farthest corner, then slipped the split rail they used for a gate into the hollows left for it in the rocks.

Josie realized the noise she had heard was coming closer, too close for her to dare expose herself trying to get back to the shelter. She slipped under the rail and back into the stable with the cattle then peeked around the rocks trying to see what was out there. The trees were mostly barren having long ago lost their leaves, all except the post oaks which still clung to their browned leaves, waiting for the spring growth to finish pushing them loose. The leaves, coupled with the dense underbrush, succeed in blocking her view of the valley. But based on the racket it seemed there must be a part of the infantry on the move. A fiery red cardinal darted out of the brush, chirping his disapproval at being disturbed.

Suddenly a single young soldier broke through the green briars, his weight supported in part by the long musket he was using for a crutch. His clothes were torn and tattered, the blue of the Federal troops. He still had a rucksack slung across his back, but he seemed almost too weak to support himself, much less any contents of the battered pack. He paused then slowly sank to his knees as though fighting his way through the brush had taken his last ounce of energy. As he slumped on to the cold ground, Josie could see the brown stain that covered his the front of his coat near his shoulder blade

Josie listened for the racket she expected from other soldiers, but as soon as the young man slipped to the ground and stopped moving, the woods became quiet again. She waited for a few minutes before leaving her hiding place, then she cautiously climbed down the hillside to the motionless figure. When she reached the body, she gingerly prodded him with the toe of her shoe, expecting to find the boy had died on the spot. Instead he suddenly gasped a deep breath and grabbed her ankle. Just as quickly his fingers loosened, and he became lifeless again. Uncertain what to do next, Josie squatted by the boy and spoke softly to him.

"Are you okay?" she whispered, knowing it was a ridiculous question even as she asked.

A moan seemed to work its way up from the soldier's chest and he returned a whispered, "No, ma'am, I'm dyin'."

"Can you get up if I help you?" Josie asked.

"I don't know." He breathed his response rather than spoke, the air rushing from his cracked, bloodied lips.

"Let me try. If we can get you up, I can take you to Mama, and maybe she can help you."

Josie gave no thought to her decision. She was aware of the war that swirled around them but had never really considered the impact on one single individual. This boy was hurt and needed help. He was barely older than Humphrey. She couldn't leave him on that cold, hard ground to die by himself.

She slipped her arm under him and helped him get slowly to his feet. With her support on one side and the musket helping him keep his balance on the other, they slowly made their way up the dried creek bank until they reached the steep, rocky path to the hide-away.

"Mama?" Josie called out. "Look at what I found!"

CHAPTER 13

ZEKE'S STORY

Josie was sitting cross legged on the dirt floor, her elbows on her knees and her chin cupped in her hands as she watched Zeke sleep.

"Don't disturb him," Addie cautioned. "He still needs a lot of rest."

"I won't wake him," Josie told her mother. "I just wonder where he came from."

At that moment the boy's eyelashes fluttered, then he slowly opened his eyes. He turned his head from side to side taking in his surroundings.

"Where am I?" he asked in a whisper.

Josie explained how he ended up in a pile of blankets on a dirt floor by the fire in their cave. Then she asked, "What's your name?"

"Zeke Edwards, Miss," he answered.

"How'd you get shot?" Josie inquired.

Addie interrupted. "Josie, let the boy get some strength back, then he can tell us all what happened.

Zeke lay next to the fire, his body fighting fever and chills as he overcame the infection that tried to set up in his shoulder. After they removed his blood-soaked coat and shirt, Addie had instructed Josie on how to care for his injuries. Josie had bathed the wounded areas in the front and back with goldenseal, amazed that he was at least lucky enough that the lead cartridge hadn't broken a bone as it passed through the softer flesh. Making a poultice of wild indigo, she pressed it against the torn flesh and wrapped it tightly, binding his arm against his chest. Then she prepared a tea with tsiyu to help control Zeke's fever. After that, they waited.

Three days passed before the fever broke. Zeke's mind cleared, and he was alert enough to talk. On that third evening, he began telling the family about the events that brought him to their hiding place.

Springfield, Missouri, March 1863

"If only Pa had not been so spiteful," Zeke began as he lay on the hard ground looking at the curious faces of the family seated around him. Then he continued with his story.

Months earlier, in March, 1863, almost a year ago, he had run away from his home in Newton County in southern Missouri, escaping to Springfield where he signed up for the military. At twelve, (but almost 13 he reminded himself), he should have been too young to enlist, but he convinced the recruiter that he was fourteen, an orphan, and wanted to help the Union somehow. He was allowed to fill out the paperwork and given a scratchy blue uniform that swallowed his small frame. Told he could only serve as a drummer or as a message runner, he had begun tapping out rhythms on any handy surface with whatever he could find to use as drumsticks. He could already run like a deer.

Pa had always been hateful and demanding of his sons. Zeke's older brothers, Zeb and Zack, had finally gotten their bellies full and left the summer before. They'd told their friends to let Ma know they were headed west to find work and adventures, and that they'd send word back to her whenever they could. They didn't leave a message for Pa. Zeke just wished they'd have taken him along, because since they left all of Pa's demands and contrariness had been aimed at him.

Pa never chewed out the little girls, Zena and Zelma, and he left Zula Belle alone as long as she was helping Mama. Zeke decided long ago Ma gave each of them Z names hoping each baby would be her last, but she just kept having them. Zelpha, Zane, and Zinnia had died when they were tiny and were buried in a small field behind the barn on their farm. Pa wouldn't let Ma pay for a plot or a proper burial at the church cemetery.

Being a soldier didn't seem so difficult. One of the older men, a private who was probably eighteen or so, got his sewing kit and helped Zeke hem up his jacket sleeves and pant legs. They managed to tack in his pants at the waist, but if it weren't for the rope belt he tightened around his middle, his breeches would be tangling up his ankles in about three steps. Once his hair started growing out and getting pretty tousled, his cap stopped sliding down over his eyes. He'd been growing pretty fast, and he hoped by really cold weather he'd fit better into the coat he'd been given.

For awhile being a soldier wasn't nearly as exciting as Zeke thought it would be. He'd missed a major engagement at Springfield back in January, but he heard a lot of stories about the battle around campfires each evening. Evening campfire was his favorite part of the day, a long day that started at sun-up each morning.

When the bugle sounded across the camp as light began to filter between the limbs of still barren trees, men began stretching and unwrapping from their blankets like moths pulling loose from their cocoons. The first chore to be tended to was stirring the coals left from the previous day's fire, then water was retrieved from a nearby creek and dipped into tin cups which were placed on the coals to boil for coffee. Most of the soldiers sliced off a piece or two of their ration of salt pork and threw it into a shared skillet to cook and eat with a piece of hard tack. A little time was allowed to tend to shaving and personal grooming, what little could be done under the circumstances, before they were called to muster.

There had been no major battles in the area since January, but some of the squads were sent out daily to watch for Confederate guerrillas that might be prowling in the area. Some small skirmishes had been reported, but most of the activity seemed to be south of the Missouri border for now.

Meantime the soldiers left in camp spent their days practicing drills, keeping their guns clean, practicing more drills, reading letters from home and writing back, or in most cases, finding the men who served as scribes for the unit to read the letters aloud to them and write home for them. Sometimes a small group would be allowed to go foraging with strict orders to not take food from any of the farm families in the area. The foragers would often return with deer, rabbits, squirrel, nuts, or later in the spring, berries. These would be added to their supper by the camp cook and shared, everyone thankful to have fresh food.

When evening came most of the soldiers contributed part of their rations to the cook, the one man in each unit who seemed to make their food somewhat edible. They always had beans or peas, often had rice, and usually had potatoes and corn cakes or biscuits. When they were lucky the rations included some kind of dried fruit, and the cook would prepare fried pies, but that was a rare treat. There was always salt pork for flavoring the beans or peas, and occasionally they had tinned meat. What kind of meat the small tins contained was always a guess. Sometimes they had hominy, pickled cabbage, or some sort of dried vegetable added to prevent scurvy. Each soldier prepared his own coffee or tea and the cook ladled out the food onto wooden trenchers.

It was during mealtime that the stories began. They usually started with battles fought, skirmishes with the enemy, acts of bravery and heroism. But from there the soldiers would began telling tales from home, sharing news from their latest letters, retelling jokes that had been laughed at before. After everyone was through eating, someone might pull out a harmonica and play a mournful melody, then someone else might sing a song or two. Occasionally several of the men would join in on some of the familiar hymns, battle cries, or love songs.

Zeke was the baby of his platoon, the newest and youngest recruit, but he was treated as an equal. The older soldiers were protective of him, but they didn't treat him as a child for which he was grateful. He sat at the back father away from the campfire during the evening meal and listened to the tales shared by his fellow warriors, longing for the day when he, too, would have tales of glory to share.

While listening to one of the stories Zeke came up with an idea that might help him get involved with more action in the war. A first sergeant William Baskett was briefly in their camp talking about Company K of Missouri's Sixth Regiment Provisional Infantry. They spent their time operating against guerrillas and didn't spend much time in camp. Zeke built up his courage and approached Sergeant Baskett.

"Sir," he said, standing at full attention and saluting smartly.

"Yes, Son?" the older man replied.

"I'm seeking information, Sir," Zeke told him, "about Company K."

"What do you want to know?"

"Is there some way I could join up? I really would like to fight, not just stay around camp practicing drills, Sir," the boy told him.

"Well, Son, you may be willing, but I think you have a problem."

"What's that?" Zeke asked.

"Company K is a mounted infantry. Each man is responsible for providing his own horse. Do you have a horse?" the soldier replied.

Zeke slumped. "No, Sir, I don't. Is there any way around that?" he asked hopefully.

"Sorry, but no. But Private, you listen here. If you are wanting to help in this war, you keep up those drills, but you also keep your eyes and ears open to anything you might do, maybe something you might not be thinking about. You're young, and battle is not a pleasant experience. There are a lot of ways you can help without having to be on the front line. You strike me as a smart lad, so use your head," the older soldier concluded.

"Thank you, Sir," Zeke said. Then he saluted smartly again, turned, and left, feeling dejected. This war was getting boring.

He had kept Sergeant Baskett's words in mind, sticking to the daily drills and routine while keeping his ears and eyes on alert for some special duty he might be able to perform. He overheard a conversation a couple of weeks later that led him in what he felt was the right direction.

"We need more couriers."

Those four words stuck in his mind, a part of a discussion between the captain and lieutenant colonel.

"We have to find someone who can find his way around unfamiliar territory and can slip around enemy encampments. These Confederate deserters keep bringing us news they could use down south, and we need more messengers to get reports to them."

Zeke went to work immediately. He borrowed some paper and a pen and started drawing maps. Visiting with other soldiers from other parts of Missouri, Kansas, Arkansas, and the Indian Territories, he quickly had a good idea of where the towns and villages were, the locations of the major rivers and streams, and what landmarks could be easily located. He had always had a good sense of direction, never once getting lost while deer or squirrel hunting in the thick woods and rolling hills of his homeland. He had learned to read the night sky from the stories his mother had told him, watching how the constellations rotated throughout the night and the seasons. He was ready to make his move.

"Captain, Sir," Zeke said, saluting smartly as always. "Can I discuss something with you?"

The captain eyed the young boy curiously. He was just a child, swallowed by the uniform that had been tacked and tied up in an attempt to fit his small frame. Smiling, he replied, "What's on your mind, Private?"

"Well, Sir, I'm too young to fight, and I'm not being of much use around here. I know you need couriers, and I think I could help with that."

The captain smirked. "Well, I admire your willingness young man, but we need someone who can find his way around, slip in and out of dangerous places, and get around fast. I'm not sure you could handle the responsibility."

81

"Sir, name a place you might send me. I will tell you how I would get there."

Surprised, the captain threw out, "Well, Fort Gibson over in the Indian Territories."

Zeke responded by describing the shortest route to the Texas Road, the supply route which then led straight to Fort Gibson.

"I'm small, I'm fast, I can read the night sky and I know the main landmarks during the day. I can ride a horse if you need me to. I grew up in the woods and don't get lost in them. I can do this if you give me a chance, Sir," Zeke told him.

Astonished, the officer looked the boy over again. "Let me give this some thought. Your determination is impressive," the captain replied.

Two days later he called the boy into his tent. "I have a message for the major stationed at Fort Scott. Get it to him and get back here. You can use one of the horses in the corral, but make sure you choose one you can handle."

That was Zeke's start as a courier.

It was late June and torrential rains were pounding the roof on the commander's tent. Inside Zeke stood at attention as the lieutenant colonel shuffled papers on his desk. This was the first time Zeke was taking orders from anyone above the rank of captain.

"Son, this one is important," he said quietly, looking up at the young soldier. "The couriers we are using are all gone on other missions. We have some news from one of the Confederate deserters, and we need to get word to Colonel Williams as soon as possible. He is leading the First Kansas Colored Infantry, and they are somewhere on the Texas Road between Fort Scott and Fort Gibson. Think you can find him?"

"Yes, Sir!" Zeke replied confidently.

"It is imperative you reach him before they get to Cabin Creek. Colonel Watie is planning on meeting up with General Cabell to attack the supply train there. Williams needs advance notice so they can be prepared."

"I'll get the message to him," Zeke promised as the officer handed him a thick envelope. Zeke wrapped it tightly in a leather pouch which he then tied under his shirt.

"You've been really reliable, soldier. If they need you down there, stay until they get things under control then get back here," the officer commanded.

Zeke nodded, then he pulled on his coat, slapped a wide brimmed hat on his head and saluted smartly. He dashed from the tent through the rain toward the corral. He already knew which horse he wanted. Old Tony had proven to be a reliable mount. He was a fast runner, didn't excite easily, and was smart enough to stand still when Zeke mounted and dismounted him. After saddling the horse and wrapping some oats in a cloth rag and tying it tightly, Zeke stopped by his barracks to tuck some supplies into his saddle bags. This trip might take a few days.

Riding steadily for eighteen hours, by mid-afternoon on June 29th Zeke finally approached the rear of the 200 wagons that made up the supply train. He quickly located Colonel Williams and gave him the dispatch. Williams halted the wagons before they reached Cabin Creek. The creek was flooded and they would have to wait for the water to recede before they could cross. Zeke used the time to catch up on his rest. He stayed at the back of the supply train, sleeping under one of the wagons.

The infantry had arrived before Cabell could get to the site with his reinforcement and join Stand Watie. Cabell had been held up on the wrong side of the Grand River by flooding. On

July second William's infantry met Watie's forces and drove them back with artillery fire and cavalry charges. Defeated, the Rebels retreated and the supply train moved on to Fort Gibson with no further problems. Zeke tied Old Tony to the back of one of the wagons and rode to the fort with them where he and his horse could rest in safety.

CHAPTER 14

COURIER

Zeke knew it would be wise to stay at Fort Gibson for a few days so that Old Tony could recover from the eighteen hour ride before they returned to Missouri. The first morning he stood at the window of the soldiers' barracks looking across the rolling hills surrounding the fort. He turned to the young private who had befriended him.

"Who are they?" he asked, nodding to the mass of people wandering about or huddling in small groups outside the walls of the fort.

"Refugees," Private Brown replied.

Donald Brown had lived on a small farm in southeast Kansas before joining Colonel Phillips regiment. Although he was only seventeen, he had already fought in several skirmishes and had been a part of the recent encounter that was now referred to as the Battle of Cabin Creek.

"Where did they come from?"

Brown told him, "They are Cherokee, Creek, Seminole, members of several different tribes that were living in the Indian Territories."

"Why did they come here?"

"For three reasons. They were seeking food, shelter, and safety. They've been caught in the fighting between the Yankees and the Rebels, and most of them have had their homes burned, their crops destroyed, and all of their livestock killed or confiscated. The Union told them to come here and they would try to protect them and provide them with some provisions."

"There's a long line that goes around the front of the fort. What are they doing?" Zeke persisted.

"Well, the supply wagons came in yesterday, and as soon as they unload all the provisions the soldiers will be needing they'll pass the rest out to the refugees. They wait in line until they can get whatever their share might be."

"Donald, you told me a lot of them are Cherokee. Seems like Colonel Watie would be looking after them."

"Ha! Not likely," the young soldier exclaimed. "If they are here, they have sided with Chief Ross and the Union, and that makes them declared enemies of Watie. Doesn't matter how old or young they are, he'll do anything to destroy them. He blames the Union for taking Cherokee land in the eastern states and moving the tribe to the territories, and he still holds John Ross responsible for the murders of his family and friends just after the removal. He has a long memory."

"I noticed there aren't any young men in the camps. Where are they?"

Brown told him, "Well, they are probably fighting with the Union somewhere. If they were with Watie's Long Rifles their families probably wouldn't be here. Some of them may have gone south to Texas or out west until the war is over just so they wouldn't have to choose sides and fight. A lot of the Indians don't feel this is their war to be involved with anyway."

Zeke looked across the expanse of thrown-together tents, shanties, and blankets that marked the boundaries of the areas claimed by families. There was little privacy, and only a few small fires dotted the area, fires shared for cooking and heating water. The women and old people shuffled around aimlessly, but the children seemed to have found games to entertain themselves in groups at the edge of the encampment. It was muddy, crowded, and forlorn, not a pleasant place to pass time.

"Thanks," he said, nodding to Private Brown. He left the barracks and roamed around the fort. The inside of the garrison was a sharp contrast to the disorder outside the log walls. The brick barracks were neat and well kept. Homes for the officers were pleasant with yards and gardens that had been tended to. There was a large, two-story white frame building that served as the hospital, as well as other stone buildings including a mess hall, chapel, and storage buildings for the supplies that were brought to the fort for redistribution. Some soldiers were drilling on an open field nearby, while others were tending to their rifles and rucksacks. They approached their duties with an urgency that projected the feeling that another battle was looming.

An unusual level of noise and excitement woke Zeke the next morning. Rolling off his cot, he looked out of the window and saw what could be a nearly a full infantry marching through the gates of the fort. Accompanying the soldiers were wagons loaded with artillery, ammunition, and other supplies. He realized Major General James G. Blunt had arrived from Kansas with his support troops. The Union did not intend to lose Fort Gibson to the Confederacy.

Zeke stayed on for two more days watching all the preparations for battle. Then, feeling useless, he stopped by Colonel Phillips headquarters and asked to speak to the officer.

"Sir," he said, saluting. "I think it is time for me to head back to Missouri. Since I'm not allowed to take part in any fighting, I am of no use here. With your permission I will plan on leaving in the morning."

"Certainly, Private, we appreciate the help you gave us. Feel free to return anytime," the colonel told him.

Zeke saluted, turned, then left for the barracks to say his farewell to Private Brown and pack his saddle bags. At daybreak he would get Old Tony from the stables. They were going home.

Zeke left Fort Gibson just as the sun rose the next morning. He soon came to the Arkansas River and turned north on the Texas Road toward Kansas. Trees towered above the road forming a green tunnel that somewhat protected Zeke from the glaring sun during the day. He had already shed his shirt, trying to escape some of the heat that beat down from the sky then rose up in waves from the ground. Another line of storm clouds forming in the west during the mid-morning had swallowed the sun. The air, thick with humidity from days of rain, was almost unbreathable. Old Tony's tail swished constantly as he attempted to keep the horse flies from settling on his back and neck long enough to bite, and Zeke slapped at mosquitoes, gnats, and other annoying insects that were drawn to his sweat-covered skin.

By noon the heat was so suffocating he made the decision to stop and rest. Finding a creek that was running bank full, a rarity this time of year, he tethered Old Tony where he could graze, then after taking a quick swim in the cool water he settled under a large maple tree to eat a dry biscuit before trying to sleep for a bit. Resting now would make it possible to keep moving well into the night when it would be cooler. After a couple of hours of fitful dozing, he finally gave up, put the saddle back on Old Tony, and they resumed their journey.

The sky was barely lit with late evening sunlight when the sound of a single rifle shot echoed through the trees. Zeke guided his horse quickly off the road and into the thick brush in the nearby woods. He sat in silence for several minutes, then hearing no further sounds of action or other soldiers, he quietly urged the animal back to the road and moved slowly toward the curve ahead. Rounding the bend, he saw a young man in Yankee-blue trousers sitting by a dead horse.

"Hello!" Zeke called.

The soldier grabbed his rifle and yelled back, "Who goes there?"

"A fellow soldier. Name's Zeke. I'm headed back to Missouri. What's happened here?" he asked, moving closer.

"Horse must'a stepped in a gopher hole. He rolled right over on me, broke my ankle I think. Broke his leg, too," the soldier answered, then paused before he continued. "Had to put him down."

"Sorry," Zeke told him. "What can I do to help?"

"Don't rightly know." The young man sat for a moment, fighting off pain. "Name's Charley, by the way. Think you can make a splint for this ankle?"

"Never done it, but I can sure try. What do I need?"

"See if you can find a couple of sticks, straight and strong. Then we'll tear up one of my shirts to tie up my leg to the sticks. I'll probably need another for a crutch."

The next few minutes the two soldiers worked together to create a support for the broken bone. But even with the splint and crutch, Charley couldn't stand. Zeke searched the area until he found enough wood to build a campfire off the road and away from Charley's horse. He made certain there was enough wood to last the night. The heat wasn't needed, but it would help keep wild creatures at bay, and they would be coming when they smelled the dead animal. Zeke pulled the saddle and tack

89

off the horse, then grabbed the soldier's saddle bag and placed all of them next to Charley.

Once Charley was settled, he asked Zeke how he came to be in Indian Territory. Zeke explained his job as courier, and told him about his stay in Fort Gibson.

"Zeke, I think I can trust you," Charley told him. "I have a packet of letters I need to get to General Blunt. I can't make it on this leg and without a horse, and they need to get to him now. Would you turn around and go back to the fort to take them to him?" Charley asked.

Zeke only paused a minute before he replied. "Let me get a couple of hours of sleep and let my horse rest, then we'll head south again. I think we can be back by noon tomorrow. I'll put you on back behind the saddle so we can get you some medical help."

"No," the soldier replied. "You send someone back when you get to the fort. It'd slow the horse down too much if he had to carry both of us. You go alone. I'll be okay."

Two hours later Zeke woke, ready to return to Fort Gibson. He made certain Charley had his rifle by his side along with ammunition that was in easy reach. He piled a few branches next to the soldier to throw on the fire to keep it burning and placed food and water next to him as well. Mounting Old Tony, he set off down a road that was only faintly lit by a sliver of moonlight.

It was midday when he once again rode through the gates of the fort. He left Old Tony at the stables and went immediately to officers' quarters to request a meeting with General Blunt. He was instead ushered into Colonel Phillips quarters. After a quick salute, he explained why he had returned to the fort and showed the colonel the packet of letters he had brought back with him. The officer accepted the letters then quickly dismissed the young private. He followed Zeke out the door and marched over to Blunt's headquarters. In a few minutes he stepped back outside and motioned for Zeke to step inside.

"Private Edwards," General Blunt said to Zeke, "I want to thank you for bringing these to me. They confirm what we had suspected, that Cabell is bringing reinforcements up to join Cooper at Honey Springs. I needed that information."

"You are welcome, Sir," Zeke replied.

"Let me ask you something." The general turned to Zeke. "Charley Taylor has been running messages for me, but I understand he is going to be out of commission for awhile. Are you critically needed with your unit in Missouri?"

"Well, Sir, not necessarily," Zeke told him.

"Then if I send word to your commander that we need you here, would you be willing to stay and serve as one of my couriers for the time being?" General Blunt requested.

"I would be honored, Sir, if you are sure to send word to Missouri. I sure wouldn't want them to think I'd deserted!" Zeke replied.

"Then it's a done deal," the general told him. "I'll have one of my men show you to your quarters."

"Yes, Sir," Zeke saluted, turned, and left the room

It seemed ironic that he had been a soldier for over a year, and for his own protection he had never been allowed to go into battle. But then as a courier, he found himself lost and alone somewhere in Indian Territory with a gunshot wound. If he had ever been assigned to a squadron or platoon, there would have been someone with him, someone to be looking for him. But that hadn't happened.

Late February 1864

"And that's how I ended up here," Zeke explained as he lay on the quilts on the floor of the cave. "I was running messages back and forth between Fort Gibson and Fort Smith for months, but a few days ago some of Watie's Long Rifles got after me. I thought if I followed the Illinois River back up from Webber's Falls, I could find a place to turn back to Fort Gibson, or Fort Blunt as they call it now. But one of the Long Rifles shot me. I kept going for awhile, but I guess I'd have died out there in the woods if you hadn't found me."

Levi stared long and hard at the young man. "You have put us in a bad position here," he said. "We've been trying to stay where the soldiers won't be aware of us, and you may have brought them close to our hiding place," Levi told him.

"Perhaps not," Zeke replied, "since it's been days since I've seen any of them. I don't know where or when I fell off Old Tony, but most of the time I've kept hidden and moving.

"How can we be sure you won't tell others about where we are when you get back to the fort?" Levi asked.

"Zeke replied, "Sir, I wouldn't do that. For starters, I don't know where I am. When you take me out of here, if you want to blindfold me I certainly wouldn't resist."

Levi nodded without answering, then turned and left the shelter. He was concerned, but not just about being discovered by Watie's soldiers. His family was near starvation, and here was one more mouth to feed. At this point he didn't know how much longer they could hold on, and he didn't know how safe it would be to leave and go back to their cabin. There just seem to be no good choices anymore, and he felt overcome with his inability to make a decision. Most of all he just wanted to take his family home, to go back to their lives before this war disrupted everything and everybody.

Levi made one choice without having to give it much thought. He would eliminate two mouths that had to be fed with one action. If Zeke was willing, he would blindfold the boy, put him on the gelding he'd found, and lead him away from their hiding place. Once they got to the wagon road Levi would give Zeke directions to Tahlequah and send him on his way. Hopefully no one would challenge the boy for riding a CSA branded horse while wearing a Union uniform. He hated losing the horse, but he couldn't find enough food to keep it well fed and didn't want the beautiful animal to starve to death.

A week passed, and Zeke gained enough strength that he started walking around outside the cave each day. He ate as little as possible, knowing he was taking food from this family who had been so kind to him. He shared what news he had of where the battles were being fought and how the war was going, news that Levi found particularly interesting.

Finally Levi took him aside and asked, "Son, are you feeling strong enough to travel? I don't want you to go before you're well enough, but if you think the horse can carry you back to Tahlequah or Fort Gibson, then for the sake of my family, I think you should leave as soon as possible."

Zeke replied, "Yes, sir, I'm much better. I can be ready to leave by tomorrow morning."

And by the time the sun cleared the horizon the next day, he was gone.

CHAPTER 15

A FAMILY DIVIDED

Mount Tabor, Texas

On a chilly evening at the end of February, Andy Humphrey strode into the small, makeshift log cabin in Mount Tabor, Texas, and collapsed on one of the benches next to a rough hewn table. His mind was focused on his sister Addie and her family that he had left behind in the Cherokee Nation. Where had they gone? He rested his elbows on the table top, his large hands covering the beard on his cheeks.

"Annie, I need to go back to Tahlequah."

Andy and Annie had been in Texas for almost three years now. Their home, not much more than a one-room shack, was still a step above the living quarters of many of their fellow refugees from the Indian Nations. Cherokee, Creek, Chickasaw, and members from numerous other tribes had settled in the area, waiting for a resolution of the Civil War that had raged in the States, eventually spilling into each of their supposedly independent territories.

Andy had followed the advice of his father-in-law, and when war broke out in the states, they began making plans to evacuate to Texas. Unlike most of those residing in the Cherokee Nation, Reverend Price foresaw that the divisiveness of the war in the east would create serious discord within the Nation as well. It soon became obvious that the Cherokee were again facing their own civil war as members of the tribe began declaring loyalty to either Chief John Ross, who supported the idea of neutrality, or to Stand Watie, who stood with the Confederacy. There was still great animosity between the two men dating back to the Removal, and they seemed to be using this war as another opportunity to settle the score.

So early in 1860, Andy's family loaded a large wagon with the possessions they felt they needed, joined Reverend Price and other families, both white and Cherokee, and began the long trek south to the safe haven called Texas.

At first the refugee camp in the Mount Tabor community had not been unpleasant. There was sufficient fresh water and food supplies. Most families found plain lumber or logs and built simple cabins for shelter, planning only to stay a few months. But the few months dragged on to many months, then years. More and more refugees arrived, fleeing the violence in the territories. But they escaped hastily and came empty handed, forced into sudden flight and arriving unprepared to care for themselves. Fresh water and food became scarce, and diseases spread through the camps. But they still felt more secure than they would have been in their homes to the north.

Annie looked at her obviously distraught husband seated at their table. "Why? Why now? There is still a lot of unrest between here and the Cherokee Nation. We have reports every week of skirmishes, and you know the Union Army is trying to push the remaining Confederate forces back to the south and east. It still isn't safe!"

"Annie, there's something wrong. Addie's family is missing. I just talked to Robert Ketcher. He had a letter from home. They told Robert's family to say hello to Addie and Levi, for them to be glad they spent the winter here instead of on their farm since it's been so cold. I started asking around, and there were a couple of other families that said they'd heard Levi had brought his family to Texas. When they didn't see them, they just assumed there was a change of plans."

"But you can't go. We need you here!" Annie objected.

"You have your father and the girls and our friends to help you with anything you might need," Andy replied sadly. "We can't both leave in case either of the boys tries to reach us here before this infernal war is over."

Annie turned to him in anger and demanded, "No! You can't just go back there and leave us here!" She grabbed her coat and stormed out the door. Andy sighed as he watched her march down the dusty road to her father's cabin. He hoped that given some time and space she would simmer down and realize he had to leave. He had to be certain his sister and her family were not in danger.

He went outside to the woodpile and gathered an armload of logs. Taking them inside, he put two sticks on the low fire they kept burning on the hearth and piled the remainder next to the fireplace. It was primitive, like everything else in this cabin, indeed, in this entire community. Gone were the days of living in the lovely, well-built home they'd had in Tahlequah, the home Annie had shared with her father before she and Andy had married. They had kept the home when Reverend Price moved to Sallisaw to help with the work of translating the Bible into Cherokee and had ended up staying there to start his own church. Now they didn't even know if their house was still standing.

Hazel and Delphia would soon be home from school. Andy and Annie had been grateful there had been that distraction for their daughters. Hazel was now teaching the lower levels when

she finished her own work, something Andy knew Addie would
be pleased to hear.

But meantime, where was Addie?

Annie shuffled back up the road, dust rising around the
hem of her skirt. The air was cooling as sunset neared, and she
pulled her coat tighter around her shoulders. Looking up, she
saw the dim light from their coal oil lantern through the cracks
in the door of their cabin. She kicked at a rock sending it off the
side of the road into the dry grass.

Hazel and Delphia are home from their classes, she thought.
*Hazel will fix some corncakes to have with those infernal beans that
have been cooking all day. I'm so tired of beans. I'm glad she's old
enough to help out 'cause I'm sure tired of doing it all.*

She sat down on the stump of a tree, one that had probably
been cut and sawed into boards for their cabin. *Rough cut*, she
thought, *like everything around here. Rough and uncivilized and
unpleasant.* She stood up, adjusted her skirt, tightened her jacket
again, then she slowly started her trek back to the cabin.

This is not how I am supposed to be living, Annie mused as
she stopped and looked at the simple wooden building which
served as their home. *I should be back in my beautiful house
with my maid helping me, hosting quilting bees, tea parties, and
fundraisers for the missions. I should be bathed and wearing a
pretty dress, not this raggedy thing.* She tugged angrily at the worn
cotton skirt swaying around her legs.

Annie's throat tightened as her eyes filled with tears. Jackson
and William should be inside laughing and talking with Andy,
teasing their little sisters, getting ready to go court some lovely
young lady, not off . . .

She shook her head slowly, not even able to complete her thought. Off where she had no idea. Her fingers lightly stroked the packet of letters she kept in her pocket. Now months old, they were the latest correspondence she'd had with her sons, her precious twin boys.

Jackson and William had not looked like twins from the time they were babies, and it soon became apparent their personalities would be different, too. Jackson was an early talker and practiced constantly. He was outgoing and never met a stranger. William was slower to talk and was quiet, letting his brother speak for both of them. He held back from people, hesitating to make friends until the person became very familiar to him. Jackson always rushed into adventures; William thought about consequences. Both boys were very bright, but Jackson seemed to just slap ideas into his mind while William studied them from several angles, letting them soak in gradually. Still, they usually got along well with each other, mixing like salt and pepper.

Until this war started.

Andy tried to discourage them from getting involved, telling them it was a war of the states, and they lived in the territories. But the passions of both the Union and the Confederacy had spilled over the boundaries of the country and into the Indian nations.

With the fervor of the Southerners, Jackson proclaimed his allegiance to the Confederacy. "The United States federal government has no right to tell the states how to manage their own affairs!" he argued. "The leaders are arrogant and believe they can dictate what is right and best for everyone based only on what they want for themselves. Look how they treated the families we know, moving them like chess pieces off their ancestral lands so they could give Indian land to white families. Then they want to tell the Southerners how to treat the Negroes?"

"You can't say you believe in slavery!" William challenged. "That goes beyond everything Father and Grandfather have taught us. No man should own another!"

"The states of the South know that," Jackson argued, "and given just a little more time they will abolish slavery without the federal government interfering, just as they need to in the Territories. Our Cherokee neighbors had slaves as well."

"But how long? And meantime, is it in anyone's real best interest for them to become two countries?" William replied. "The United States will become weak and subject to assaults from European nations. The states need each other, each and every one! Only by remaining united can they remain strong."

And the arguments raged back and forth in their tiny cabin, in small gatherings in the streets, even in the church yard after Sunday services. Annie was thunderstruck when William waited until just after breakfast one sunny summer morning to announce that he was leaving for Springfield, Missouri, where he would be signing up with the Union Army. Despite her tears and Andy's pleading, he was packed and gone before lunch. With no chance of their recovering from that blow, Jackson angrily declared that he was leaving for Little Rock, Arkansas, where he would find the closest place to enlist with the Confederates.

Annie was devastated. By nightfall both of her boys were gone.

She stroked the packet of letters again as she pushed open the door and slowly walked back into her house. Just as she had expected, Hazel had supper on the table, the usual beans with corncakes. She slipped off her coat, and after hanging it on a nail behind the door, she reluctantly joined her family at the table.

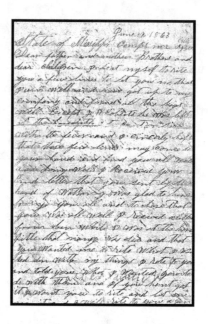

CHAPTER 16

LETTERS FROM THE CAMPS

"Annie, we have got to talk." Andy spoke quietly, hoping to not wake his daughters who were sleeping in the narrow loft he had built under the eaves for their bedding. "There is a supply train leaving for Fort Blunt tomorrow—I still want to call it Fort Gibson—and I have been hired on as a driver. This way I can make us a little money while I'm finding out what has happened to Addie's family."

"You mean *you* have got to talk," Annie replied tersely. "As usual, this is not a decision *we* are making. You have decided what you are going to do, and it's all pretend, acting as if whatever I say has any influence."

Annie sat leaning on the table with her chin on her arms while staring into the fire. Her back was turned to Andy as she continued.

"It doesn't seem to matter to you that you are leaving me here with an old man and two young girls to look after. I have no choice about going with you, because if the boys come here looking for us, someone needs to be here for them."

Andy sat in silence, unsure of how to proceed. Finally he replied, "But Annie, Addie is all the family that I have left on my side. If she needs help, I need to be there for her. You knew when we married that I had made that promise to her. I'll be back as quickly as possible. You aren't in any danger here, and you know you'll be looked after by your father and his congregation. If the situation were reversed and he was the one missing, you'd want to know what happened to him. So please don't be angry."

Annie sat in stubborn silence, still facing the fire. Andy stepped out to the porch, loading his arms with firewood. He returned to the small room and piled the dried logs onto the fire.

"It's time for bed, Annie. Are you going to join me?" Receiving no response, Andy finally told her, "Well, good night, then. Maybe we can talk tomorrow." He made his way to the back of the cabin, pulled aside the quilt that separated their sleeping area from the rest of the room, and crawled into their bed, pulling the blanket over his shoulders.

Annie sat in the silence for awhile, then she reached into her pocket and carefully pulled out the packet of letters. She gently extracted the last two, the most recent she had received from Jackson and William. *It has been such a long time*, she thought.

She moved next to the fire, settling in Andy's chair where there would be light enough to read.

June 12, 1863
Camps near city Yazoo
State of Mississippi

Dear father, mother, and dear sisters,
I seat myself to rite you a few lines to let you no that I am well and have got up to my company and found all the boys well. Except J.J. Roberts he was left at the hospital at Canton sick with the fever. I sincerely hope that these few lines may come to your hands and find you all well. I received your kind letter that you sent by the hand of Watson. I was glad to hear from you all and to hear that you was all well. I received a letter from Ben while I was at the hospital that Grandfather had been ill and I want you to rite and let me no that he is all right now. I would also want to no that my brother William is well, even though we are on opposite sides of this war.
You wanted to no something about the times here. Times is very hard here and everything high. Corn is worth ten dollars per bushel, bacon a dollar per pound, tobacco is 2.50 per plug, and chickens is seling from 2 to 3 dollars apiece. Eggs 2 dollars per dozen, butter 3 dollars. I am needing some close very bad. I want a pair of pants mighty but there ain't no chance to get them to me and I will have to do without them. If I see any chance to get any from home I will write to you and you can send them to me. Our fare is very bad here.

We don't get any to eat but beef and meal and the beef is very poor and the meal is coarse as homily and we get about enuff to do us 2 meals for a day's rations. We neither get sugar, rice, molasses, not potatoes nor nothing of the kind and we hant got any tents and we have to take everything as they come. We are here and we don't no when we will have to leave for we are expecting to leave every hour and we don't no where we will go too. But I recon if the Yankees don't come here to us in a few days we will make a move on them towards Vicksburg for they are fighting every day up about Vicksburg and have been for about 3 weaks. But I think we will whip them there though Old Grant has a very large force there. But Johnson has amany a man here in his army. I think we will have some very hard fighting to do but I may be mistaken.

I will bring my letter to a close. Give my love and respects to all inquiring friends, so no more at present, and I remain your son and brother untill death.

Jackson Humphrey

Annie smiled as she read the letter, recalling that Jackson had never felt the need to be concerned about his spelling. Her smile faded as she reached the reference to Vicksburg. They had since heard that Johnson had not taken his troops to Vicksburg but instead had moved toward Atlanta and had battled Sherman's army. Where Jackson had been that past ten months was a mystery.

She then unfolded the other, smaller letter.

June 23, 1863
Vicksburg
State of Mississippi

Dear Mother, Father, and sweet Sisters,

It is with a little hope that I have a moment of solitude so that I may write a note to you. It seems as soon as I pull out my pen, one of the men from my company is standing with hat in hand, eyes pleading, requesting that I write a missive to his loved ones. I have, it seems, become the scribe for our company, a position which I do not mind except that it gives me little time to write to my own loved ones.

I am doing well, or as well as can be expected during a time of war. Our rations are decent, but certainly not enough to make us fat and robust. Uniforms are showing signs of wear, and I am sad to report that it is not unusual for men to take the shoes off soldiers who have been killed in battle if such shoes are in decent condition. Many of us are nigh on barefoot with the wear our boots have taken from long marches.

I have, thankfully, seen little of the battlefield myself. The officers have also found my level of education beneficial to them, and I find myself serving as general clerk. These duties are not what I had anticipated when I enlisted, but there are many jobs that must be done in wartime and not all involve weapons.

Our company has now joined many other in what is being referred to as the Siege of Vicksburg. We have been here for several weeks with surrender from

Pemberton expected any day now. This will divide the Confederacy and will hopefully soon bring an end to this seemingly endless conflict.

I hear word of each battle, fearful that my brother is on the other side of the line. Although we have our personal battles, I pray that he remains safe and unharmed and comes home to you soon.

I must now close as duty calls. With love and deepest affection,

Your son and brother,
William Humphrey

This was the last letter they had received from William. Both boys seemed to have vanished after the fall of Vicksburg. For awhile Annie had been frantic because there had been no letters, but then word reached them how the lines of communication had become so disrupted that little correspondence was getting to anyone. Now she felt smothered in a dark cloak of sadness, fearful that she might never hear from her sons again, might never know if or where they had fallen.

Folding the letters carefully, she returned them to her pocket. She quickly undressed and slipped her worn nightgown over her head, then she deftly twisted her hair into a tight braid. Sliding quietly under the pile of blankets, Annie turned her back to Andy and finally fell into restless sleep.

Chapter 17

LEAVING TEXAS

"Father?"

Andy turned from his kneeling position on the hearth before the fire. He had been quietly placing small broken branches on the coals that remained from the night before, hoping to coax the dried wood into blazes to warm the chilly cabin.

"Yes, Hazel. You are up and about early this morning," he whispered to his older daughter.

"When you get the fire burning, can we step outside for a few minutes? I'd like to visit with you and don't want to disturb Mother or Delphia."

"All right," Andy replied, then blew softly on the coals until a small flame licked at the dry tinder. He rose, helped Hazel with her cloak, then pulled on his coat and followed her out the door.

The sun was just rising, but the tents and cabins in the refugee settlement were still shaded by giant shadows cast by the lofty pine trees that flanked the clearing. A light fog mixed with thin plumes of smoke trailing from chimneys then drifted to the south in a light morning breeze. It was chilly. Spring was just around the corner, but winter had not yet fully released its grip on north Texas.

For a moment, Andy stood with his daughter in the quiet of the early morning and they watched the day as it began to unfold.

"Father, I didn't mean to eavesdrop but I heard you and Mother arguing last night," Hazel told him.

"Oh," Andy replied. "We didn't mean to disturb you."

"That all right," Hazel told him. "I just wanted you to know I understand why you need to leave. I want you to know I'll take care of Mother while you are gone. May I make a suggestion?"

Andy turned to his daughter and smiled. "Of course," he told her.

"Grandfather should move in here with us while you are away. We could go to his cabin, but Del and I have our sleeping loft already built here, and he doesn't have a place for us. He can help Mother with her chores, and she can look after his needs without having to go to his house. And Papa," Hazel paused.

Andy smiled at her again, please with the use of the affectionate name rather than the formal "Father" she usually used. "Yes?" he asked.

"Mother will get over her snit. She always does. I just hope she doesn't wait until after you have to leave." Hazel returned her father's smile.

"Mother just feels she has to have a man around, and if Grandfather is here she will be comfortable with that. Del and I aren't babies anymore, so we can take care of ourselves and help her whenever she needs us. I'm just concerned about what has happened to Aunt Addie's family."

"So am I, Hazel," Andy nodded in agreement, "so am I." He paused then continued, "Do you not want to have a man around when you get older?"

"Papa, I want to become a teacher first, like Aunt Addie. I don't want to depend on a man to support me. If there is to be someone in my life, I want it to be a man I choose because I care about him, not someone I need because I cannot take care of myself. And besides," she added sadly, "look around, Papa. This war is killing so many of the young men. When it is finally over, there won't be enough decent men of marriageable age to go around. I certainly don't want to marry some old man just to become his caretaker."

Andy looked at his daughter in surprise. He hadn't realized she would give such thought to marriage, but then she was approaching the age where a lot of young women did marry. Her attitude make him proud although the reality of what she said about the war brought an ache to his heart. He slipped his arm across her shoulder and they returned to their cabin.

The smell of frying pork drifted from the cabin as they walked up the hard-packed path to the door. Andy saw the Dutch oven, glowing red coals piled on top, as soon as he entered the house. It sat next to the open fireplace where Annie was removing strips of bacon from the skillet. She looked up as they came through the door.

"I didn't want you to go away hungry. There'll be enough biscuits so that you won't have to wait until they have the mess ready, at least for the first few days you are on the road."

Andy smiled, hoping this was Annie's way of apologizing for her anger.

"Thank you," he replied.

Delphia joined them around the small table, and they shared the last meal they would have together for the foreseeable future. When breakfast was over, Andy put the last of the belongings he was taking with him into his rucksack, then he gave his daughters a hug. Annie walked out the door with him, and at the end of the path he gathered her in his arms.

"I'll come back safe and as quickly as I can," he promised her. "And when I have a chance I'll send word to you of where I am and what news I've found by anyone we meet coming this way."

"Take care, Andy," Annie replied, "and I'll send messages by way of anyone going to Tahlequah or Fort Gibson. I hope you find Addie's family out of harm's way." She handed him a package of biscuits wrapped in a soft cloth. Then she continued.

"I knew when we married that you would always be responsible to some degree for Addie as well as for our family. I'm sorry if it seems selfish, but I just really do feel your place is here with us. But since you feel you must go, then go, but be safe and come back soon."

Andy kissed her on top of her bowed head, then turned down the road toward the line of wagons. They were loaded and ready to start the long and arduous drive to Fort Gibson.

CHAPTER 18

CARAVAN

The caravan of wagons left Mount Tabor and turned northwest. It would have been a more direct route to go due north, but those who had migrated to Texas from the Indian Territories knew there was a range of mountains between them that would have proved difficult, if not impossible, to cross with the wagons. So they began making their way to the Colbert community in the Choctaw Nation where the Indians operated ferries that could take them across the Red River.

The wagon train was accompanied by a platoon of Union soldiers for protection. Although control of the Indian territories had been fairly well reclaimed by the northern armies, Stan Watie still commanded an active presence with his Long Rifles in the area between Fort Smith and the Texas border. It was not unusual to hear of skirmishes between the Indians and Union soldiers along the Texas Road, and they did not want the contents of their wagons falling into Confederate hands.

February ended, and the constant threat of spring rains kept the wagon train moving night and day as steadily as possible. Where the ground was rocky or hard packed they moved quickly. But with the weight of the wagons rain, or even the deep thawing of the ground, quickly turned the roads into a quagmire. It became almost impossible for the horses and mules to move the heavily loaded vehicles. More than once their passage was halted as the men dragged out shovels to dig down to solid ground and free the wheels from the mud.

Most of the drivers knew Andy as they had lived in or near Mount Tabor, and they knew that he often served as preacher when his father-in-law needed a substitute. They asked him to conduct brief church services Sunday while they were on the move, a request he was willing to grant. Because time was precious, the services started with a hymn, followed by a prayer, and then a brief reading from the Bible which constituted the ritual.

They had only been gone six days before Andy was called on to conduct a different kind of service. One of the soldiers guarding the wagons had neglected to firmly tighten the cinch on his saddle, and it slipped to one side, throwing him from his horse's back. It would have been a simple fall, but he struck the back of his head on a large rock as he hit the ground. The blow killed him instantly. Andy performed a brief funeral service and the young soldier was buried off the side of the road. The grave was covered with stones so his family might be able to locate him if they ever tried. Andy knew that would be unlikely, that the boy would just become another of the dead who disappeared from his family never to be heard from again.

The caravan crossed the Red River at Colbert and turned back northeast. They reached Boggy Depot just as one of many spring rains hit, making further progress impossible until the water drained from the road. It was there that a horseback rider caught up with the wagons, bringing letters from Mount Tabor. Andy smiled as he unfolded the note that Annie had sent, and his smile widened as he read the salutation:

My dearest husband,

Andy was relieved to know that Annie seemed to sincerely have gotten over her snit, just as Hazel had predicted. He was even more delighted at her news.

> *I hope this letter finds you quickly and that your trip has gone well. I have wonderful news to report. Just two days after you left, I saw a strange man walking up the path to our door. He was thin and unshaven, with unkempt hair and a worn Union uniform. However it only took a moment for me to realize I was looking at our own William. He has come back, and has returned safe and unharmed physically although I fear his spirit is damaged. I will let him tell you his story upon your return to Mount Tabor.*
>
> *Forgive me for being brief, but the rider is leaving soon, and I hope to get this to him in hopes he catches you somewhere along the road. Father, the girls, and I are doing well.*
>
> *With much affection,*
> *Annie*

Two days later the roads had dried enough for the wagons move and they were traveling north again.

CHAPTER 19

LETTERS FROM HOME

Late March 1864

Four weeks passed before the wagon train finally pulled through the gates of Fort Gibson late one spring afternoon. Andy looked with sorrow at the encampments around the fort knowing there was a good chance he might know many of the refugees, former neighbors or customers in Humphrey's Mercantile. He was ready to put behind him the stress of potential attacks from Long Rifles or bushwhackers as well as the daily trials of dealing with wheels mired in mud. The rainy season was not a good time to travel with heavily laden wagons.

They were directed to an area where their cargo would be unloaded. Then one of the soldiers led them to a large stone building that served as barracks. They climbed the stairs and walked down the wide porch to an end room which had been assigned to the drivers. Each of them threw his rucksack on a cot then headed to the mess hall the soldier had pointed out on their way to the barracks. The drivers had decided that sleep would come easier and last longer following a hot meal.

As Andy walked across the commons area he realized he had not even noticed how beautiful the countryside had become. Spring had officially arrived, and several of the officers homes had crocus, hyacinths, and bright yellow jonquils blooming in the ladies' gardens. Splashes of the slender, yellow forsythia plants and blood-red japonica blossoms hedged the gardens. Brush strokes of pale green stretched across the hillsides that were dotted with white blossoms of the dogwood and purple-pink of redbud trees. The air had been washed clean by the recent rains, and as Andy took a deep breath he realized how happy he was to be near home again.

The exhausted drivers sat together at one of the dining tables quietly enjoying the first really hot, fresh meal they had eaten in weeks. They were served only brown beans, fried potatoes and cornbread but enjoyed the food as much as they might a seven course feast. There was little conversation in the group until a soldier walked over to them. They knew by the eagle on his epaulettes and the rectangular patch on his coat that he was a colonel. One of the older drivers motioned for him to join them, but he stood at attention.

"Colonel Griffin, gentlemen," he said in introduction. "You may be interested in the mail which has been forwarded to you. It is being held in the commissary, and you may pick it up whenever you wish," he told them. "Which of you is Andy Humphrey?" he asked.

Andy held his hand up. "I am."

"The major would like to see you after you have eaten and slept for awhile. He asked that I let you know it is no rush, just at your convenience," the colonel told him.

"All right," Andy replied. Although his curiosity almost got the best of him, he added, "Tell him I will see him first thing in the morning."

"Yes, Sir. And thanks to all of you for your efforts in getting these supplies to us. They are greatly needed and deeply appreciated." He turned on his heel and left them to finish their meal.

The men finished eating quickly, each of them anxious to get to the commissary to see if there was a letter from a loved one waiting for him. Andy was relieved and delighted to find a packet of letters tied with string. He waited patiently until returning to his cot in the barracks to open the packet. Once he was finally settled in, he began reading.

He first selected letters from Hazel and Delphia. Hazel assured him that Annie was doing well, that having William back had helped cure her of most of the sadness she had felt from Andy's departure. Delphia wrote about school and activities around the camp. He anxiously opened the large bundle of letters Annie had sent. He easily recognized Jackson's handwriting on many of them in addition to two from Annie. He open one from Annie first.

Andy,

We do so miss you terribly. It is taking all my patience waiting for your return and hope it will be soon. It is with some hesitation that I send the enclosed letters for fear they might be damaged or lost before they reach you. However, they are from Jackson, and he has so much information I did not want to try to retell all of it. Some were posted even before we received his letter from Yazoo City.

We are all well. One of the members of Father's congregation brought us a good supply of firewood. Winter is almost past, but it is still needed for cooking and to keep the night chill at bay. Father insists on stacking it under the overhang, a long and tedious job for him now as he can only handle one or two logs at a time. He is wanting to feel helpful, though, so I do not argue. He seems to be enjoying his stay here, and we are so thankful just to have his presence.

I am so hoping you find Addie and her family soon, and they are all well. Please come home as soon as possible.

Annie

Andy then turned his attention to the enclosed pages, the letters from Jackson.

November 13 1862, Abbeville Missisipi

Dear Mother, Father and little Sisters,

If you received my last you are eager to hear what has become of me by this time. I hope that you have been receiving my letters. The mail service is very irregular. When last I wrote we were on the eve of a retreat. Since then however all has been more quiet and we are camped at Abbeville near Oxford and about 20 miles south of Holly Springs which you can find on the map of Missisipi. It has become common for us to retret of late though I hope our last retret has been completed as our army began to advance again yesterday morning. Our Regiment will remain here till we get our horses, we are the guards for this place.

Human suffering is so common here that a dying man elicits no more attention here than a dead hog would there. Yesterday a man died on the platform at the depot. It was reported to the provost who said to the one that told him "Go bury him then" and turned off. He laid there till today when 6 men dug a hole, rapped the man in a blanket, put him in and covered him up.

Men care very little for anything here. They boast of their stealing and think it shows shrewdness. Last night one of my Regiment stole about a bushel of potatoes while guarding them. Remember I am not messing with Tom or Bill or John but others. This is the greatest place in the world to learn human nature. Men that at home were respectible are the greatest rogues.

Often this kind of life is tiresome to me. Though I mingel with thousands I pass my happiest times in solitude. While the camps are alive with aparent mirth I wander off in the woods sit down by a tree and my mind dwells upon the misrie of our people. Sometimes I almost wish I had never lived to see this day. Yet it is my destiny as well as duty to suffer my part. Therefore I quiet myself and prepare to meet my doom. I say doom because out of a company of 87 men 12 months ago we have now only 20 alive here for duty. Then what will be the result of 12 months more? How many will escape? Will one, and shall I be that one?

You may suppose from this that I am downhearted but not so. I think less about home than ever being better contented than before. I have more on which to live my income being greater. My life is in no greater danger than before. The greatest hardship to this mode of life is the filth of camps. There has hardly been a time since we crossed the Missisipi River that the Regiment has been clear of body vermin. We are forced to march through clouds of dust for weeks without clean clothes with nothing but our water buckets to wash in and no pot vessels suitable to boil in as our pot vessels are always lost on a retreat. Bread, meat, and sugar is our fare and when cooked by men that have marched all day and are tired no panes are taken. Dirt and filth makes one part of the meal.

Our blankets are thrown down in the dust day after day and night after night. No one thinks of washing a blanket. Thus amid dirt, filth and exposure who is able to withstand it? We meet the enemy to end our existence or conquer a peace. You will suppose that I am tired and want to return. I am tired of the war but have no desire to return while it rages. I would be glad to see home for a short time but I could not be content there long. You may be surprised to know that I still want to improve my mind. I still desire my education yet the battlefield is my place while growing up. I should hope that I gain fame from the battlefield. These dreams are whatever they may be and may become true, yet I seek not fame. Advancement is before me, rank easily obtained though I will not be a seeker. I have no doubt but that soon I will be called to the 1st Lieutenancy of the company as there is nothing between me and that position according to the rule of promotion. I will not receive it unless it is the choice of the company and then I will be most content with the survival of my men.

Andy laid the letter on his cot. He sat, saddened, imagining the horrors his son must be facing. Only twenty surviving from an original eighty-seven, only one out of every four. And the filth must be abhorrent for a boy who had a mother who always kept his home and clothes so clean for him. Andy stretched out on the cot, holding the letters next to his heart as he drifted into a fitful slumber.

CHAPTER 20

JACKSON'S STORY

Andy awoke just as the sun began its climb above the horizon. There was a soft glow across the encampment, and tendrils of fog wove in and out of the trees that edged the nearby woods. He started to stretch then realized he still had Jackson's letters spread across his chest. As he began to gather them he remembered the message from Major Potts about a meeting. Curious, he folded the letters and bound them again with the twine then placed them in his rucksack. Tossing it across his shoulder, he headed once again for the mess hall. After a quick breakfast of biscuits with gravy and scrambled eggs, he headed to the officers' quarters.

"Andy Humphrey here to see Major Potts at his request," Andy told the young soldier stationed at one of the doors along the lengthy log structure.

"I will see if he is available," was the brusque reply. Walking down the porch, the soldier stepped through an opening at the far end, disappearing inside. He soon returned and motioned for Andy to follow him. Andy was ushered into a spacious room with a stone fireplace at one end. Windows lined the front wall overlooking the porch. On the opposite side of the room, a makeshift table covered with papers was pushed up against a solid log wall covered by several maps. At the end opposite the fireplace was a desk, cluttered with stained, half empty coffee mugs and more piles of papers. A portrait of President Lincoln hung over the desk, and the wrinkled face with his despondent eyes overlooked all activity in the room. The major looked up at Andy. His face showed exhaustion, and a deep sadness was reflected in his eyes as well. It was obvious that he, too, was ready for this long war to end.

"Mr. Humphrey, so glad you came by," the major said as he stood with hand outstretched.

Andy shook the major's hand as he asked, "How can I be of service, sir?"

Major Potts sat back down and motioned for Andy to be seated in the cane bottom chair across from him.

"We are grateful for all of your efforts in getting those supplies to us. We are feeding so many people and have gotten quite low on provisions. The ammunition you brought will help us defend the fort. However, most of the conflicts have moved east and this area is now fairly safe."

He nodded at the cup on his desk and asked with a smile, "Would you care for coffee? It will keep you awake for the rest of the day." Andy shook his head in polite refusal, and the major took a sip of the thick, black brew then leaned back in his chair.

"We have a small situation you might be able to help us with," he told Andy.

"And what would that situation be?"

"It is my understanding that you have served as a minister to your convoy in the miles between here and Texas, that you acted in the same capacity while living at Mount Tabor."

"Yes, sir, I did. But I wouldn't want you to get the impression I am a fully ordained pastor. I have helped my father-in-law in emergencies when he was ill or away and could not tend to his usual Sunday services."

Major Potts nodded. "That's fine and it's good enough for what we need. The minister who has been serving the soldiers stationed here has gone to Fort Smith to check on his mother who is ill, and we just need someone who is willing to conduct a Sunday church service tomorrow."

"If there is nobody else available, then I would be glad to help. But I can't give communion or offer much in the way of counseling services. I am just not qualified for those types of duties," Andy replied.

"That's fine. Then we will count on seeing you at the chapel tomorrow morning, say about nine o'clock?"

"That will be fine. Anything in particular you want addressed?"

"No, just something uplifting to help these men face another week during this infernal war," the major answered. He stood, and Andy did likewise.

"I'll let you get back to your duties," Andy said as they shook hands in farewell. He picked up his rucksack and headed back to his space in the barracks.

Sunday services were over. Andy had kept them brief, finding songs and Bible verses that were optimistic and encouraging. He kept his sermon concise, hoping to persuade the congregation of mostly soldiers to keep their faith in the trying times of war. After the service he accepted an invitation to join Major Potts and his family for dinner. He slipped away as soon as possible, anxious to continue reading the letters Annie had sent him.

July 1, 1863 near Little Rock, Arkansas

Dear Mother, Father and sweet Sisters,

I hope this finds you safe and well. Your letters are not finding there way to me, so I can only hope that Grandfather is now well and you have had word from William that he is also safe and well.

When last I wrote we were camped in Yazoo City near Vicksburg certain we would soon be doing battle there. However, those in charge decided to take our little unit east instede. It seems we have done more marching than actual fighting which is perhaps a good thing. As small as our little unit is, we are just moved from place to place like pieces on a chess board, never staying in one area long enough to be involved in battle.

This may soon change. We have gotten word that Lee is taking his army north into Union territory in the State of Pensilvana. We have decided to make our way toward the north and east in hopes of joining one of the fighting forces. A deciding victory there could mean a faster conclusion to this seemingly endless War.

"Mr. Humphrey?" A young soldier stood at attention at the door of Andy's room in the barracks.

"Yes, sir. What can I do for you?" Andy replied.

"There is a soldier in our infirmary who is asking to see you. The colonel wouldn't disturb you, but the boy claims his name is Jackson Humphrey, says he is your son."

Andy's head whipped around; the soldier now had his complete attention. "Please take me to him. I'll obviously know if he is being truthful or not."

Andy followed the soldier's long stride to the infirmary, his mind whirling with questions, hoping he would soon have the answers. *Would this be his Jackson? How did he get here? Why was he in the infirmary?*

Once inside the three-storied white frame building he was led to the back of a large open room. Cots were lined up along the wall, most occupied by soldiers sporting bandages on some part of their bodies. On the last cot at the end of the room lay an emaciated, bearded man. It only took a moment for Andy to look behind the beard and long shaggy hair to see the face of his son. He bent down and embraced the boy in a gentle hug, receiving one in return. Then he pulled a rickety three-legged stool next to the cot to hear Jackson's story.

Jackson told him, "When they told me the morning services were given by an Andy Humphrey, I knew it had to be you. So I asked one of the nurses to send for you."

"The last letter I read, in fact I just finished reading, said you were headed toward Gettysburg to join forces there. What happened? How did you end up here in Fort Gibson?" Andy asked.

Jackson sighed and leaned back against the wall, propping his head against one arm.

"It was a calamity. The remains of our squad, our little band of 20 soldiers, had gotten to the far side of Tennessee when we began meeting troops, just scattered bunches of soldiers, coming back south. They told of great losses of men killed or wounded on the battlefield at Gettysburg, how Lee had to retreat. So we turned back, too, planning to return to Little Rock in hopes of finding some sort of leadership and the remains of another squad to join so we could attach to some platoon. We figured that was the only way we could still stay a part of this war, still stay on some sort of payroll and get fed.

"Papa, it was a nightmare, those men, those skeletons coming back from battle. They were so gaunt, so hollow-eyed. It was like their spirits had just left them. Some barely shuffled along supported by hand-whittled crutches, bandages on their heads, or slings holding their arms. Some of them were still soldiers, still traveling with their squadrons. Others, well, they were deserters and didn't really care who knew it. All they wanted was to get back home, to see if they had a home left, to check on their families, their folks and wives and children. And there were families, too, who had given up and were trying to escape west or get to Texas, anywhere but where the fighting might continue."

Jackson halted. He seemed to need a moment for his thoughts to catch up to his voice. Shaking his head slowly, he continued.

"But what we really had to watch out for were roaming bands of bandits. They had no respect for anybody, supported no cause. They attacked without warning, killed without reason, took what they wanted, and rode off without fear of retribution."

In the silence that followed Jackson's little speech, Andy looked up, really seeing his son. The boy was thin and unkempt, his hair long and shaggy, his beard untrimmed, but he had made an effort of sorts to keep as clean as possible. Then Andy looked at what he had not wanted to see. The blanket that covered Jackson dipped to the cot, clear to the cot, below his left knee where his leg should have been holding it up. He looked up to Jackson's face and met the boy's eyes.

"What happened? Or are you ready to tell me about it yet?" he asked.

Jackson paused, then replied, "Let's go to the mess hall. We can talk after breakfast."

Andy didn't tell his son that he'd already eaten. He held out his hand to help the boy pull himself up from the cot and keep his balance as he reached for a pair of crutches leaning against the wall. Andy had not let his mind register the existence of the crutches or what they might mean. They were crudely made with rags wrapped around the arm and hand braces to cushion them somewhat. As they moved toward the door Andy noticed that in spite of his thinness, Jackson's arms and shoulders were well-muscled, a result of supporting a good portion of his weight.

Jackson finished breakfast, then they wandered outside, finally settling on a crude wooden bench beneath an old pecan tree. Jackson laid the crutches on the seat next to him and rubbed the muscle on his upper leg. They both sat back and enjoyed the warmth of the spring sunshine.

"Father, why didn't anyone in our family ever talk about evil?" the boy asked.

"Why Jackson, what do you mean? Your grandfather preached about good and evil almost every Sunday, and your mother and I have always tried to teach you about right and wrong," Andy replied.

"No, Father, you're talking about sin, about the Ten Commandments and all that. I mean evil. This war has taught me about killing, about men and women who will steal to stay alive. I've seen married men cavorting with prostitutes, and most of us neglected to remember the Sabbath. But these are sins, things I think we can ask to be forgiven for, and we will be. But I never knew about real evil."

"Do you want to tell me about it, son?" Andy asked quietly.

"Want to? No, but I think I need to," Jackson replied. "We were moving slow. It was last August, hot, humid. There was twenty of us to begin with, the same twenty that had been together for weeks. But as the days dragged on five fellas gave up hope and split off, heading back to where ever they called home. Two turned toward Memphis hoping to find work since we hadn't been paid in weeks. Two more got sick with the dysentery, too sick to travel, and they insisted we go on to Little Rock. They said they'd join us when they got better. That's the last we saw of either of them. Ol' Mac Johnson, he was messin' around the creek fillin' his canteen and got bit by a big water moccasin and was dead in twenty-four hours.

"The ten of us that was left, well, one evening in early September we caught up with this little bunch of people trying to dig a hole at the side of the road. I guess you'd call them refugees. It was just an old man, a couple of women, two half-grown kids, and a little tyke barely big enough to walk. The old man, Homer, told us the women had lost their husbands in the war. One also had a son killed, just a kid. Soldiers had burned their houses and fields then taken all the livestock they had left. They were headed to Texas, hoping to get far away from the fighting where they might be able to find a way start over, to survive. The old man's wife had just died and they were wanting to bury her, so we stopped to help. For some reason ol' Vance McGooden took a shine right off to one of the ladies, the mother of the little one, and volunteered us as escorts as far as Little Rock.

"Anyway, they was about to starve out, so we slowed down even more so we could help them out a bit. We could still hunt and could get a rabbit or squirrel and maybe even a deer every now and then. Someone always seemed to know what plants we could eat, or leaves, berries, roots, whatever. We didn't eat great, but at least we weren't starvin'.

"Turned out the arrangement worked pretty well. We did a little hunting, and the ladies fixed food as best they could with what supplies we had. They also washed our clothes, so we looked and smelled a lot better. One of them even had a pair of scissors and did a little barbering. They slowed us down some, but we really weren't in that much of a hurry. Fall was comin' and we just wanted to be farther south before the cold settled in."

Jackson stopped. He took a deep breath and let it out slowly, staring at the toe of his well-worn boot. He hesitated a moment then continued.

"We camped near a creek one evening, and I decided before the weather got any colder I wanted to get a good bath without all the horseplay when the other fellas were around. So I waited until late and went down to clean up. I wanted to be good and dry before I put my clothes back on, so I sat by the creek awhile just enjoying the night sounds.

"By the time I got back to camp, everyone had settled in for the evening, and all the spots around the fire were taken. It wasn't that cool yet, but it just always felt safer near those blazes. I was pretty irritated because no one thought of leaving room for me, and I was feeling sort of sorry for myself. But I'd seen a big root from an oak tree growing out of the ground up the path a bit, making just a nice size hollow that I could crawl into and keep safe, at least safer than I 'd be sprawled out there on the ground away from the fire. So that's where I went.

"It was about daybreak when it happened, so sudden that at first I thought I was dreaming some kind of nightmare. There was musket fire, and screams, and men yellin'. Took me a second to clear the cobwebs, get out of that hole in the ground, and grab my gun. By then it was almost over. It was a random gang of bandits out to pillage our campsite. We didn't have anything of value 'cept our horses so they just took them. Then just out of meanness they tried to kill everyone, even the children, even that baby. One of them fired a shot, just a haphazard thing, as he rode out of camp. That's the one that hit me in the leg. I got off easy."

Jackson paused, his shoulders slumped, then near tears, he continued.

"Papa, I didn't get wounded in battle defending the Southern Cause I believed in. I wasn't hurt coming to the rescue of the men in my unit. I wasn't even able to save those poor people who thought they were safe with us. I was too late, too slow to help anyone. McGooden died trying to save his lady friend and her baby but it didn't help. Six of our men were killed, two of us were injured, the other two managed to find cover and were okay. The other woman and one of the older kids both got shot but weren't hurt bad. The old man and the other kid were dead, too.

"Loy and Sam buried the dead, patched the rest of us up best they could, then we started hobbling our way on to Little Rock. We got to where some supply wagons were moving that way, and they picked us up. By the time we got to the city my leg had gangrene and had to be sawed off. I stayed in the hospital for awhile, don't know where the others went. When I got where I could travel, I made my way west back here. I think they took me in to be certain I wasn't some sort of a spy. Then I got sick again, so they put me here in the infirmary."

The silence was heavy when Jackson stopped talking. At first Andy didn't know what words his son needed for comfort, so he reached out and put his hand gently on his arm.

"Don't fault yourself for not saving those people. You tried to help, but you just weren't in a position where you could. And it cost you your leg for at least trying."

"I don't care about this war anymore," the boy said softly. "I don't care who wins or loses. I just want to go home."

"Okay," Andy replied.

"Okay?" Jackson echoed.

"Certainly. I don't think the Confederacy wants you anymore; they wouldn't consider you a deserter now. And I've not heard anything about your being a prisoner of war. So let me find a wagon that's headed to Tahlequah, and we'll get out of here and get you home."

CHAPTER 21

WILLIAM'S STORY

Mount Tabor, Texas

Annie stared with unseeing eyes at the plain pine coffin resting at the front of the alter at the front of the brush arbor that had served as a church for over three years. March winds whispered through the tall pine trees surrounded the simple structure on three sides and the open area to the east was partially occupied by a small cemetery just north of Mount Tabor. A discreet mound of new earth along the far edge gave mute testimony as to where the coffin would be placed following the service.

Thoughts whirled in Annie's mind. Things were happening too fast, coming at her like blows from an angry fist. Father had just gone out to bring in a single piece of firewood, a simple action. How he had tripped and fallen was still unclear, but when he fell he broke his hip. Neighbors had helped her move him into her larger, more comfortable bed rather than place him on his narrow cot. She had tried to make him comfortable, but within a week he had developed pneumonia, and he had just faded away. He died on Sunday morning with her at his bedside feeling totally helpless.

Even before all this Annie had been having long conversations with William, conversations with a totally unexpected and unwelcome topic. William planned to leave.

'I can't stay, Mother." He had been unyielding in his determination.

"But why, Will?" she had begged. "You are safe here, surrounded by family and friends. We need you. There is plenty for you to do. You're far away from the war now, so why leave?"

"Not far enough. I can't sleep at night. I can't get those memories out of my head. Any sudden noise makes my heart race. I just need to be completely away, not where I still hear of battles, and who is missing or fighting off in some far-flung state. I don't want to be where the war is still the main topic of conversation, the main thought in everybody's minds."

"But where do you want to go?"

"I keep hearing about California. It's supposed to be a great place to live with lots of work a man can get. They say the trip across the desert can be rough, but that it's really worth it. And it is really, really far away from the United States, the Confederacy, and the Territories. Just a place to start all over. That's what I want."

"Will, what happened to you? Can you tell me? Can you talk about it?"

Will sat silent for a few minutes with his hands in his lap, studying his fingers. "I'm not really meant to be a soldier." He finally said.

"I was all right as long as I was in the tents, writing letters and orders, working with the officers, separated from the fighting. But then late one afternoon, just as the sun was setting, the fighting came to me when the camp and then the soldiers outside the officers' tent were attacked. I rushed out and saw Captain Ryan trying to handle a Gatlin gun by himself. His partner was lying at his feet with a bullet in his head." He paused and turned to his mother.

"Do you know what a Gatlin gun is? It's a perfect killing machine, a repeating gun that doesn't have to be reloaded one bullet at a time. Just by instinct I stepped up and helped Ryan, fed the ammunition into the gun while he shot and shot and shot. It was only later that I saw what he had shot. We had protected the officers and the ground was littered with mangled bodies. But they weren't just bodies, Mother, they were boys and young men and old ones, men with families back home who'd never see them again, never even know where their remains were buried. And I thought of Jackson. It was then I turned cold, like my feelings just clicked off, and I turned against everything this war represented. I just left a few days later, one deserter among many from what I hear."

Annie had sat stunned. Eventually her chores called her, but her mind was busier than her hands. Later that evening she had asked William to take a walk with her.

"Will, are you trying to get away from your sisters and me?" she asked hesitantly.

"No!" he replied emphatically. "You are what I will miss the most. I can only hope to return to see you or have you make the trip west to see me."

"Then Will, I have an idea you may find shocking. Let us go with you to California. Your father can decide on his own whether to join us or stay in Tahlequah. I have no desire to go back there. The city is destroyed, so we have no business or church to return to. There is no telling what condition our house has been left in." Annie continued, "I, too, want a new beginning. Somehow I think your sisters might have a better chance of finding worthy beaus there than anyone here or back in the Cherokee Nation."

"But Mother," Will replied, "what if Father doesn't join us?"

"That will be his decision. He didn't hesitate to leave us to go back to look for Addie and her family. Let him do what he wants. I made the trip to the Territories with my father against my wishes, and I made the trip to Texas out of fear, but this time I want to leave with you and go where I want to go. And Will," she paused, "I don't plan to stand in your way when the time comes that you find a lady of your own. Just stay with us until we get settled, then we will be able to make it on our own."

"Mother," Will answered slowly, "I'm not giving you an answer right now. I want you to think this over. How would you feel if you leave then find out that Jackson came looking for you? You should realize that the towns in the west are uncivilized and pretty wild. I might have to find a job that takes me away from any home for long periods at a time and would not be around to protect you and my sisters. Think awhile, talk to the girls, and we'll discuss it again in a few days."

CHAPTER 22

TAHLEQUAH, INDIAN TERRITORY

It was about noontime two weeks later when the wagons from Fort Gibson pulled to a halt in front of Fishinghawk's Blacksmith and Livery Stable. Clouds still hung low in the April sky, but there was no more rain falling. The convoy had been delayed several times from the effects of heavy downpours on dirt roads, time taken digging wagon wheels out after they had sunk to their axels in mud.

Andy stepped from the driver's seat and shook water from his hat. He turned to give Jackson a hand, helping him off the wagon. Andy tied the horses to the old log rail in front of the rundown building as Jackson retrieved his crutches from under the seat. Then they headed into the dark, musty interior looking for the owner.

"Fishinghawk, you here?" he called. "It's Andy Humphrey."

Andy heard the plop as a shovel full of muck was thrown from a back stall, then a voice hollered back, "Andy Humphrey! Well I'll be!" Then a tall skinny Cherokee man pushed his way through the half door of the horse stall, set a shovel to one side, and slowly shuffled up the alley between the stalls. He wiped his hand on his britches as he approached the men, then held it out, reaching for a handshake. Andy grabbed his hand with both of his, glad to see an old friend.

"What are you doing back in these here parts?" the old man asked. "Have you come back home to stay? We'd sure be happy to see you start up that store of yourn agin."

"Well, thanks, Jessie, but I've got other things on my mind first. Maybe you can help me out," he replied.

"Come on back here outta this barn," the old man said. "The air's fresher, and it's a bit drier. We can sit and chew the fat a bit. Got some coffee in the pot, too, if you're wantin' a cup." He turned to Jackson, looking him up and down. "Growed a bit, ain't you, Boy. Looks like you had a little problem. Guess you been off fightin' somewheres. Welcome back home, Son," he finished as he motioned them into a small room at the back of the building.

Jessie pointed to a couple of cane back chairs, and Andy and Jackson sat down while he poured them each a mug of thick black coffee. The look they exchanged said clearly, "Can we really drink this?" but they knew they had to try. It was not coffee but chicory, and it was all they could do to not choke on the strong, bitter taste.

Jessie sat down on a cot that obviously served as a bed, sofa, and closet, then said, "Now, what're you needin'?"

"I'm looking for Addie and Levi." Andy went on to explain how several people had thought his sister's family had come to

Texas to join his, but they hadn't seen them. No one they had heard from who was still in the Tahlequah area seem to be able to account for their whereabouts either.

"Well," Jessie paused as he took a swig of the thick black brew, "think I can help you there."

Andy sat up straighter, hopeful at the response. "Really? What can you tell me?" he asked.

"Well, several weeks ago, back in January I guess it was, Levi stopped by here to get some moonshine."

"Moonshine!" Andy exclaimed.

"Yep, but it t'warnt fer him. He's getting it for that little boy, Evan I think he said," Jessie continued. He took another sip of his coffee then went on. "We were in a bad cold spell, and seems the boy got caught outside. Levi thought he was gonna lose some fingers and toes. He slipped into town here looking for medicine, and Aelie Glory sent him by here to get some moonshine to knock the boy out while they did what they had to do."

"Oh, poor Evan," Andy said. Then after a moment he asked, "You mentioned Aelie. Is she still in town? I guess Levi visited with her. Did he happen to tell you where his family is?"

"Slow down, Son!" Jessie said. "Yes, Aelie is still here, and it's pretty clear Levi talked to her since she sent him by here. But I have no idea where his family is staying. I don't think anyone has seen them for months, though. I'd bet they've been hidin' out somewheres to keep Levi or the boys from bein' hauled off to the army. Both sides have been pretty bad about grabbin' up anyone they think can handle a gun."

"Hiding sounds pretty likely then," Andy replied. "I guess I need to go talk to Aelie. Can you tell me where to find her? Does she still live in the same house?"

Jessie reminded him of the directions to Aelie's house, then Andy turned to Jackson.

"Son, you stay here and help with the horses then get some rest. I'll go find Aelie and see what she knows. I'll get back here as quick as I can, hopefully before sundown."

Jackson nodded in agreement. He knew that with the crutches he would slow his father down, and he knew his father would be in a rush after weeks waiting to get this close to finding Addie. Jackson said his good-byes and left to tend to the animals as Andy turned and started toward town.

Andy stayed off to the side of the muddy road, walking on the grass as he made his way into the remains of the settlement. So much of the town was gone, and Andy's heart grew heavy when he recognized the steps that had once led up to Humphrey's Mercantile. He had heard of the fires, but hearing didn't have the same impact as actually seeing the damage. Without conscious thought, he began calculating what it would take to rebuild the business.

He turned west and was soon climbing the hill that would lead him to Aelie's home. The path to her front door was so overgrown with weeds, some dead from the previous fall and some green shoots from this spring, that he almost missed it. Pushing his way up the trail he reached the door and knocked firmly.

"Aelie," he called. "This is Andy Humphrey. Are you home?"

He heard shuffling noises inside and a moment later the door opened just a crack.

"Andy Humphrey, is that really you?" a soft voice asked.

"Yes, Aelie, this is Andy. I've come to ask about Levi and Addie," he answered her.

The door swung open wider but not as wide as the smile on Aelie's face.

"Come in, come in," she called out cheerfully. "How nice to see you."

Andy entered the house and Aelie closed the door behind him. He immediately noticed the darkness. He realized Aelie lived in continual night and could function well in the darkened room, but it was going to take a bit for his eyes to adjust so that he could move about.

"How are you, Aelie?" he asked the tiny Cherokee woman.

"I'm doing well, Andy. Please find a chair and be seated. Then tell me what's all this about Levi and Addie."

Once again Andy went through his story of trying to locate his sister and her family. Then he explained how he came to Tahlequah with Jackson, and how Jessie Fishinghawk had told him to come see her.

"Well, of course," she replied. "I have all the information you need. But first let me get us a cup of sassafras tea and some cookies. I don't often have a chance to serve guests, and I just took a notion this morning to do some baking. Can't do much since there's not much to work with, but I rustled up a little something."

Andy sat, restlessly waiting for Aelie to return from the tiny kitchen. He was thirsty and hungry, but he was even hungrier for information. However, he could not be rude enough to refuse the lady's offer of refreshments.

"Thank you," he said as Aelie returned with a platter holding two cups of hot beverage and several ginger snaps. "I have to admit I'm a little surprised that you have sweetener," he told her.

"One of my brothers found some cane last fall. He made some molasses, and he brought me some tins full. We store all our supplies here in my cellar. The soldiers never think to ask, or even to search for food in my house. They assume I am helpless," she finished with an impish smile.

"Now, let me pass on the message that Levi left with me." She proceeded to give Andy the directions to the hiding place where Addie's family could be found. They weren't completely clear, but Andy felt they would get him close enough he could locate his sister, Levi, and their children.

"I just hope to find them alive and well. I'm especially concerned about little Evan," he added.

"I understand," Aelie said. "I hope," she paused. "Well, I hope Levi didn't have to cut off much, and that he healed quickly. Poor child."

Less than an hour later Andy left Aelie's house with more hope than he had felt in weeks. He headed back to the blacksmith shop resisting the urge to race down the hill in the evening shadows. Finally he had a good idea where to find his sister and her family.

"Jessie?" he called as he pulled open the heavy door of the stables. "Are you here? Is Jackson still about?"

"Come on it," Jessie hollered from the back of the building. "We're just settlin' in for the night."

Andy found his way between the stalls to the small room where Jessie and Jackson were passing time until he got back. Jessie had stirred up a pan of wild onions and scrambled eggs and had a stack of cornbread slices waiting for Andy to return for supper. He passed out three bowls and spoons, and they ate while Andy repeated the information Aelie had shared with him.

"Jackson, Aelie asked if you would come board with her for a few days while I go check on Levi and Addie. She needs some help around her place, and she'd be willing to feed you and provide a place for you to sleep while I'm gone. Would you be interested?" Andy asked.

Jackson replied without hesitation. "Of course! I don't know how much help I can be, but I guess you told her that I don't get around so good. But that would give me something to do while I wait for you."

"Good. Then that's settled." He turned to Jessie and asked, "If it wouldn't be too much bother, could we bed down in the stables here tonight? I plan to get up at daybreak so I might be able to find Addie before dark. It'll be a good hike, and I may have to look around a bit before I can figure out exactly where they are."

Jessie replied, "No problem. Glad to share the space. And I think I can save you some time." He motioned to the back stall of the stables. "I have an old nag here that a soldier-boy left quite awhile ago. Don't think he's comin' back for her. If you want to borrow her for a few days, I think she'll made a good ride for you. That'd get you where you're going a lot faster, but I wouldn't expect a race horse outta her."

Andy grinned from ear to ear. "Why Jessie, thanks so much. I'll take you up on that offer. I'll get her back to you as soon as I can. I hate to ask after such a generous offer, but do you have a saddle and some tack I could borrow as well?"

Stone faced, Jessie replied, "Nope, you'll just have to ride 'er bareback like us Indians do." Then he smiled and continued, "Course I do. Soldier left that stuff, too. You can just take it all. Let's get it tonight so you can be ready to leave as soon as possible in the morning."

They piled the saddle, blanket, and bridle next to the stall where the mare was peacefully chewing on a mouthful of straw. Then Jackson and Andy tossed some hay in the empty stall next to the mare and spread their blankets across it. Telling Jessie good night, they stretched out hoping for a good night's rest.

CHAPTER 23
FINDING ADDIE'S FAMILY

Andy was extremely thankful to have the mare to ride, but he soon realized Jessie was more than a little right about her not being a race horse.

"Giddy-up, Stirrup!" he encouraged, but the mare just plodded ahead at a steady but slow pace.

Stirrup, he though. *What a name for a horse!* She seemed to be well bred, and Andy suspected she was probably once upon a time a beloved pet of some wealthy family. At least she hadn't been left to starve or be slaughtered just for meanness in this crazy war.

The miles gradually passed by as Andy rode down the once familiar road. Since it had been seldom traveled in many months, the ruts were covered over with weeds, and no effort had been made to fill the pot holes that would have made a rough ride for a wagon or buggy. He was saddened to see the burned out remains of some of the buildings that had once been homes to families he had known, but he was glad to see an occasional thin plume of white smoke rising in the distance, a sign that there were still some outposts of life in the desolate countryside.

Just past noon he reached the point in the road where Aelie had told him he would need to turn into the woods. He guided Stirrup off the familiar ruts and into a creek bordered by woods on one side and a bluff on the other. He followed the creek bed as it wound its way up the hillside then urged the mare out of the shallow stream and into the woods when he neared the peak of the hill. Stirrup fought her way through the brambles and blackberry vines before coming to a clearing that was made of several large, flat, moss covered lime stones just as Aelie described. At this point Andy knew he was almost to Addie's hiding place—if she and her family were still there. Skirting the stones, he found where another small wet-weather stream was flowing down the hill. He stopped and began calling.

"Addie! Levi! It's Andy. Are you there?"

His voice seemed to hang in the air, caught in the early pale green leaves of the trees surrounding him. Crossing the stream, he continued toward the overhang he could barely see through the trees. He reined in the mare again and sat quietly in the saddle, listening for any human sound. At first he only heard bird songs and the rustle of leaves as a gentle spring breeze blew through the trees. Then he heard a weak voice call, "Andy?"

"Yes! It's Andy!" he shouted back and turned the mare toward the voice. He punched her in the ribs with his heels, hoping to encourage her into faster gait, but she just ambled through the brush in the direction he guided her. Within moments, he saw a skeletal figure walking toward him through the brush. He realized the gaunt figure was Levi.

Andy dismounted and grabbed the claw-like hand of his brother-in-law.

"Levi, I am so glad to see you," he told him.

"Well, Andy, I'm glad to see you, too, but what in heaven's name are you doing here? And how did you find us?" he asked.

"I'm looking for you and Addie and the children!" Andy exclaimed. "We've all been so worried about you when no one heard from you for such a long time. I decided I'd better come find you. How long have you been here?"

"Too long," Levi replied, shaking his head sadly. "Too long. We started hiding last fall after I escaped the soldiers again, and we started worrying about Humphrey and Josie. It's been a long, hard winter, and we still don't know when it'll be safe to go back."

"Are they okay?" Andy asked. "Is my sister all right? And the children?"

"Near on starvation," Levi replied sadly. "We done the best we could to find food, but it was real scarce during the winter months. Evan like to froze in a snow storm, lost two fingers and his little toes."

"Yes, I know a little about that," Andy told him. "That's how I found you. I talked to Aelie, and she told me you'd left directions here in case someone came looking for you. Thank goodness you did!"

"Well, let's get you up here to the shelter. I know Addie will be delighted to see you. Don't let on to them that you see how bad they all look. Now that spring's here, we can find more food and start filling out a bit," Levi assured him.

They began trudging up the hillside where Andy saw a pile of rocks. A little face peeped from behind the rocks, then another. There was a slight rustle before four bodies came rushing down the hillside toward them.

"Papa, who's this?"

"Uncle Andy, is that you?"

Suddenly he was surrounded by little arms giving him welcoming hugs.

"Children," Levi ordered, "mind your manners. Say 'hello' to your Uncle Andy."

Suddenly shy, the children ducked their heads and murmured polite, "Hello, Uncle Andy. It's so good to see you."

As they backed up and stood still he tried to recognize each of them. He hope the shock of their appearance didn't show on his face. The healthy, rosy-cheeked children he remember had been replaced by these emaciated, skeletal little beings who looked too weak to even be walking.

"You must be Nicholas," he said to young boy close to him.

"No!" he exclaimed. "I'm Evan. Susie and Josie are up with Mother.

"Oh my," Andy replied, "I can't believe how much taller you have gotten since I saw you last! Then you must be Melly, and you are Nicholas, and," pausing to look almost eye to eye at the young man standing next to Levi, "you must be Humphrey. You have all grown up. Three years does make a difference!" he added sadly.

"Let's get back to your mother," Levi ordered, and the children followed as they once again started up the hillside.

Just as they reached the opening of the shelter, Addie came out followed by Josie and Susie. She stood with tears sliding down her cheeks as she stared at her brother. She opened her arms and he stepped into them for a long awaited embrace. Susie grabbed her mother's skirt and sucked her thumb ferociously as she stared at the unknown stranger.

Addie stepped out of the embrace, and Andy knelt to the little girl.

"Susie, I am your Uncle Andy, your mama's brother. You know, like Nicholas is your brother, and Evan and Humphrey. I've just been gone a long time. It is nice to finally see you." Then he held out his hand. Susie timidly reached out and took it.

"All right, everybody, let's get a comfortable spot to sit and do a little catching up," Levi commanded. "Andy, you go first. Tell us about Annie and the children, then we'll tell you how we ended up here."

After a couple of hours spent exchanging stories, Levi turned to Andy and asked, "What now?"

Andy replied, "It's time for you to go home."

CHAPTER 24

GOING HOME

The smell of frying bacon woke Andy. He had bedded down for the night with Addie's family in their shelter. It felt cold and damp to him, and he wondered how they had tolerated this place for over half a year. He was thankful he had brought extra food with him so they could have breakfast. Addie was cooking wild rice with dried apples and slices of bacon as he rolled out of his blanket.

After breakfast, which the children had eaten with unbridled enthusiasm, Josie and Humphrey stayed close by eavesdropping on the adults as the other children wandered away to find something more interesting to do. Andy had begun telling Addie and Levi war stories, how the battles were going, where the armies were. It was a difficult chore convincing Levi that it would be safer and much better for his family to be back at their homestead now with a roof over their heads. That was, of course, unless it had been a victim of fire or vandals.

"Stand Watie has been pushed to the southern part of the territories," he assured Levi. "Starting in February Colonel Phillips led his troops from Fort Gibson to the Texas border telling his men to make their footsteps 'fierce and terrible'. He warned the tribes ahead of him to surrender before he destroyed them. By the time he passed, many Indians as well as whites who had supported the Confederacy had been killed. So there is very little chance anyone would be around to cause you problems now."

Addie looked at her husband. "We've got to get out of here, Levi," she said softly. "The children are starving. They may stand a better chance if we get back to where we might find food more easily. If we can find seeds, we can even get a garden planted again. They need to get out from the dampness in the cave. It wasn't so bad in the winter, but now that the spring rains have started," she paused, then stopped, shaking her head.

"I thought this was the best thing for all of us," he replied sadly.

"It was! It was at the time!" Addie insisted. "But hopefully that time has passed, and it is safe enough for us to go back home. We will just have to stay alert to any signs that there is anyone still around who would want to take you or Humphrey away."

"Then we'll do it. Let's go," he agreed. Addie wrapped her arms around his back and gave him a gentle hug.

"I'll get the girls to help me start gathering up what is still usable, what's worth taking back. You get the boys to help you with the livestock."

"Livestock?" Andy asked. "You managed to keep animals alive with you?"

"Yes," Levi replied. "We still have the cow, one hen, and one rooster. Sad to say we had to kill the calf and the other chickens to keep from starving. It's been a rough winter. Don't know where we'll find a bull so we can start another herd, but that's a worry for another day."

"Tell you what I'll do," Andy said. "While you are taking care of gathering up your things here, I'll get back on this mare and ride over to your place to see what's left. Now that I know where you are, I can find my way back. That way you won't be faced with any surprises when you get there . . ."

"Sounds good to me. We'll just expect the worst and hope for the best. But we won't wait for you to return. When we get ready, we'll go ahead and start that way," Levi told him.

Andy quickly saddled the mare. He slipped his foot into the stirrup and threw his leg over the saddle. "I'll be back as fast as I can. I won't stay at your place, just take a quick look around. When I return, I'll take the children horseback a couple at a time so they won't have to walk so far."

"We'll meet you as soon as possible," Levi responded. He turned and yelled for the younger children to come to him. "I have a surprise," he called to them as they got closer. "We're going home."

There wasn't much to gather up to take back. Addie discarded most of the bedding which had become worn and molded from the dampness of the cave. It was the same for much of their clothing; what little they had brought had not fared well over the winter. Pots and pans, some dishes, a few books that had been saved from mildew, and a few tools were all that were worth salvaging. Andy had not been gone long before they had their meager belongings gathered and were ready start the trip back home. The burdens were much lighter than when they had made the reverse trip in October which was a blessing because they lacked the strength they had in the fall.

"We'll leave now," Levi told Addie quietly, "so we can take a lot of rest stops along the way. The little ones will need them," he said, nodding toward Susie and Nicholas. "Hopefully Andy won't be long and they can get that horseback ride."

Slowly they followed Levi up the hill away from the shelter, no longer fearing the noise they might be making. As they reached the mossy flat limestones on the top of the hill, they turned and looked back through the trees. They could barely see the refuge which had sheltered them for six months, keeping them hidden from the dangers of the war that raged so close by. Then they turned and began their trek through the woods toward home.

CHAPTER 25

HELLO AGAIN

Zeke Returns

Andy made the ride back to the farm quickly, covering in less than half an hour what had taken his sister's family an hour and a half on their fastest trip six months earlier as they were going to the cave. However, he cut over the hill and straight through the woods, unconcerned about covering his tracks on the rocks of the creek bed that wound up the hollow. Stirrup was better than he could have been at pushing her way through the new growth of briars and scrub brush that had begun sprouting in the spring weather.

He reached the road and would have galloped the final quarter of a mile to the house if Stirrup had been willing. When they finally crested the hill on the east side of the farm, Andy realized there was a small plume of white smoke drifting upward from the chimney at side of the house, disappearing in the midday light. He stopped, considering his options in dealing with squatters who apparently had set up their home in Addie's house.

He led the horse to the end of the path and draped the reins across a stout limb of a cloud-white dogwood tree next to the road. Then he began calling, "Hello? Hello? Who's there?" and waiting for a reply. None came. Moments passed before he saw the small face of a young girl peek from the front window then pull back in hiding.

He tried again as he slowly walked up the path to the steps. "Hello? My name is Andy Humphrey. This is my sister's family's house. I need to visit with whoever's in there." Reaching the steps, he rested his foot on the lowest one and waited. Then he heard voices and quickly realized they were from young girls. He heard one insisting, "But he's not a soldier. He doesn't have on a uniform!"

He couldn't hear the reply, but a moment later the front door was pulled back just a crack. At the same time he heard the bang as the back door closed.

"What'cha want, Mister?" a young girl asked. By her voice he guessed her to be about eleven or twelve.

"Hello," he replied. "My name is Mr. Humphrey, and this house belongs to my sister. She and her family have been gone, but they are coming back here this afternoon. They're going to need their home back."

"Wait just a minute, Mister Humphrey," she told him. "My sister has gone down to the garden to get my brother. He can talk to you." Then she shut the door.

Andy leaned back against the post supporting the sloping roof of the porch. He looked around, taking in what he saw of Annie's home. Except for the missing split-rail fence, most things looked pretty much in order. Weeds had begun growing in the yard, weeds that would have been yanked out by his sister, but the buildings all seemed to be intact.

A tall, slender, tow-haired boy came around the end of the cabin. He held out his hand to Andy.

"Hello, Sir," he said. "How can I help you?"

"Sorry, Son," Andy replied, "But I think I need to be asking the questions. This isn't your house. You're going to need to leave because my sister and her husband, who have been away, will be arriving shortly and plan to settle back in their home. Who are you anyway, and how did you end up here?"

"Well, sir," the young man replied, "my name is Zeke Edwards, and that's kind of a long story. Come inside if you don't mind taking a few minutes, and I'll fill you in."

Early March, 1864

Levi would have been mad as an old wet hen if he'd realized his attempts at concealing their hiding place from Zeke were all in vain. He'd blindfolded Zeke then helped the boy mount the CSA horse that had stayed with them. Levi led them away from the cave, meandering aimlessly through the woods, until they finally reached the wagon road that led to Park Hill and on to Fort Gibson. At the road Levi allowed Zeke to remove the cover from his eyes. What he didn't realize that the sense of direction Zeke had that had made him such a reliable courier enabled the boy to estimate fairly closely where they had been. But he kept his mouth shut about it because he didn't want to concern the family who had befriended him, and he certainly had no intentions of giving away their whereabouts to anyone.

Zeke stayed horseback until he reached Fort Gibson, concerned the entire trip that someone would notice the discrepancy between his Union uniform and the CSA brand on the gelding he was riding. But he rode unhindered. The travelers he met all seemed focused on their own destinations and weren't concerned with him or his business.

Darkness had fallen before he guided the gelding between the wide gates of the fort. He dismounted slowly, still careful of his damaged left shoulder. He led the horse to the stables and turned him over to one of the stable hands, giving strict instructions to brush and feed the animal before putting him in a stall or pen for the night.

After seeing that the horse was tended to, Zeke found his way to the mess hall. Supper had long been served, but he went to the back to the kitchen where the cooks were finishing their clean up for the night. He talked them into a plate of biscuits and cold sausage gravy. It was hard not to take pity on this skinny, injured, and so-young soldier. Finishing his meal, he walked to the bunk house and found an empty cot where he lay down and immediately fell into a deep sleep.

The next morning he went directly to the officers quarters to speak to Colonel Phillips. When he arrived at the commanding officer's headquarters, he waited until the Colonel could see him. He entered the large room then stood at attention inside the door.

"Colonel Phillips, Sir" he said briskly, slowly raising his arm in salute.

"Private Edwards!" the Colonel replied in surprise. "We thought you were dead. One of our scouting parties found Tony, and you were nowhere around. Figured you were captured or got shot and didn't make it."

"For awhile I thought I was dead, too, Sir," Zeke replied. "But I had some help, and I'm back to report for duty. I have a little problem with my left shoulder here, but it's on the mend, and I don't think it'll slow me down. At least, not much."

Shaking his head, the Colonel looked at the boy with respect.

"Son, I admire your spirit, but I'm discharging you and sending you home. You've been a good soldier and a great help, but you're wounded, and I can't in good conscience put you back on any kind of active duty. You have taken care of your responsibilities, done your share in bringing an end to this conflict, now you have permission to go back to your family."

Zeke looked at him with sad eyes. "But I don't want to go back."

"Private Edwards, that's not a request, that's an order. You are hereby relieved of any future obligations. Shoot, Boy, you were too young for us to be using you in the first place! You just knew what you were doing so well we took advantage of it. Now, go home. That's a command. You're dismissed." And the Colonel stood up.

Zeke stepped back and saluted once again. He turned to leave but hesitated then asked over his shoulder, "Can I hitch a ride on a supply wagon toward Missouri until I at least get close to home? I've got a good horse, but it has a CSA brand on it. That's a long story, but it makes me a little nervous riding it. I think I'd be best off leaving him here."

"Yes, son, you do that. Stay here until you feel rested and get some food in your belly. You look like you could use it. Then head north. We have things pretty well under control here, partly thanks to you."

Zeke saluted a final time then left to find out when a supply train would be headed toward Missouri.

Two weeks later Zeke was hiking the narrow roads that wound through the foothills of the Ozarks into southwest Missouri. Although it was the rainy season, the supply train had made good time since they were traveling empty. They had moved north on the Texas Road from Fort Gibson in the Cherokee Nation then turned east into Missouri, headed for supplies and ammunition in Springfield. Zeke left the wagons behind shortly after they crossed the Missouri border.

CHAPTER 26
RESCUE

Racine, Missouri

Riding in the wagons had given Zeke time to heal and put on a little weight. He knew once he left the convoy by late March he'd be on foot and would have to look out for his own meals. The wagon master had allowed him to pack a few items in his rucksack, so he had some tins of meat, a little corn meal, some hard tack, and a small container of coffee. He hoped to supplement those meager rations with fresh meat if he could kill a squirrel or rabbit or catch a fish in one of the many fresh water streams that flowed through the area.

Although the days were warm, the nights were still chilly so he traveled as much as possible in the dark, taking naps in the warm afternoons so he could keep moving after the sun set. He headed for the small village of Racine in southwest Missouri. There wasn't much there, just a blacksmith, a mercantile, a saloon, the Methodist Church, and a few houses scattered along the dusty road that meandered through the town. This was the closest settlement to his father's farm that was just two miles out of town, and he hoped to get news of his family there without having to get too close to home.

He reached his destination midday after four days of hiking. He stopped, letting his eyes follow the ruts that passed for a road to where a wagon was tied in front of Bode's Mercantile.

The only other signs of life in the village were two nags tied to the hitching post next to the saloon. The town was as he remembered, the forest rising above it, hugging the edges like fortress walls. Forsythia and japonica were blossoming in several yards, and yellow topped jonquils brightened the edges of ragged wooden steps leading to the warped porches of unpainted wood frame houses.

He walked up the steps and across the wide porch to the heavy wooden door of the mercantile. He yanked the leather handle which served as a door knob, opened the door, and paused before entering the darkened, overheated room. It took a moment for his eyes to adjust to the shadowed interior of the store. When he stepped inside he saw three elderly men sitting in cane back chairs pulled up close to a glowing potbellied stove. They turned slowly to him and looked him up and down. Then a short, rotund German man waddled from behind the counter left of the stove.

"My lands," he said in surprise. "It's Zeke Edwards if I'm not mistaken."

Zeke held out his hand to the older man and replied, "Yes, Sir, Mr. Bode, it's me."

"Well, Son, we thought you was dead and buried by now. But then, your brothers disappeared and we ain't never heard nuthin' about them neither."

"Oh," Zeke replied, disappointed. He wanted further information about the rest of his family so he asked, "Do you have word of my folks? Have you seen my sisters recently?"

"You probably know your ol' man is more likely to be seen at the saloon than in here or at church," Mr. Bode replied, "but when he does bring the girls into town they come in to do the little shopping he allows."

"How are they? And how about Mama? Does he let her come in, too?"

Bode looked at him sadly. "I'm sorry, Zeke. Didn't you know?"

"Know what?" the boy replied, confused.

"Your mama done passed away."

Speechless, Zeke sat down in an empty cane back chair. He put his elbows on his knees, hiding his face in his hands. Finally he looked back up at Mr. Bode and asked, "How?"

"Well, Son, the way your Pa told it she was birthin' another baby and after it came she just didn't stop bleedin'. She just bled out. The baby didn't make it neither."

"And of course he wouldn't have sent for the doctor, wouldn't give someone a chance to save her," Zeke responded angrily.

"No," was the simple answer.

"What about the girls? How are my sisters?"

"Well, after your Ma died I guess he got pretty hard on Zula Belle, expected her to do all the work your Ma did. Somehow she started sneakin' off to see that Ritter boy and before anyone knew it they were gone, took off west from what the rumors say."

"That just leaves the little ones, just Zena and Zelma out there with him." Zeke sat quietly for a moment. "I wonder how hard he's being on them now."

"Can't tell you that, son, but I do know when they come in here they never look too happy. In fact, they never look up from the floor, and I don't know the last time I heard one of them speak."

"That's over," Zeke said harshly. He rose, and moving quickly around the store, he picked some staples from the shelves and stacked them on the counter. Thankful for the money from his service with the Union Army, he paid for his purchases and had Mr. Bode wrap them tightly. He loaded them into his rucksack, swung it across his shoulder, and nodding a brief good-bye, he stalked out the door.

Zeke hiked the familiar road to his father's house which was hidden from the main road by a quarter mile of scrub brush growing under the taller pine, elm, and oak trees. He followed the narrow path that led to the cabin but left it before he reached the ramshackle structure that had never seen a bit of repair. He settled behind a stand of sumac growing close to the ground, and from there he watched the house. It was sundown before he saw his Pa saddle the swayback mule and ride up the same path Zeke had just covered, going the opposite direction toward town.

He slipped up the path to the front door and let himself inside, calling to the girls. "Zena! Zelma! Come here. It's me, Zeke."

Two skinny girls, much too small for their ages, crept down the ladder that lead to the sleeping loft. Seeing it was really their missing older brother, they walked to him, heads bowed, and gave him timid hugs.

"Do you have shoes?" Zeke asked.

Zena shook her head.

"How about some other clothes and coats?"

She shook her head again.

"Do you have a favorite toy? I'm taking you with me, and you need to go get it if you have one."

Once more, eyes downcast, Zena shook her head.

"Zena," Zeke told his little sister, "you can talk to me. You don't have to just shake your head."

She glanced up at him and whispered, "You won't hit me?"

Feeling as though someone had punched him in the stomach, Zeke gently pushed her hair away from her face, only then seeing the finger marks across her cheek. "No, baby girl, I won't hit you. Ever," he answered.

Zeke knew he had two choices. He could stay and confront his father, challenge him on the way he had treated his mother and sisters. Or he could get them away quickly and take them where they wouldn't be found. He opted for the second idea, knowing that although he'd rather stay and beat his Pa to a pulp, it would be better for the girls if they would just leave. So he took their hands and said simply, "Let's go."

Zeke headed back toward Racine, keeping to the main road until they got close to the little village. He knew his father would stay late at the saloon and would probably not check on the girls when he staggered in. Zeke figured they had all night to make their escape and get as far away as possible. He also knew the girls needed shoes and warm clothes. Tough as their feet had become, he couldn't have them walking long distances or late into the night unless they had warm clothing. So they were going back to Bode's Mercantile.

Like many business owners, Mr. Bode lived above his store. Zeke climbed the steps and knocked loudly on the door. The old man finally opened it slightly, peeking sleepily through the narrow crack.

"Zeke!" he exclaimed. "What in Heaven's name do you want at this time of night?"

"Mr. Bode, I need help, and I need you to keep a confidence," he replied.

"What's going on, boy?"

"I've got to get my sisters away from here, and they've got to have some clothes. You know I've got money since I paid you today. I need to get some things now, tonight, so we can be long gone before daybreak."

Mr. Bode understood without being told the details exactly what Zeke was doing, so he grabbed his breeches, pulled them over his long johns, then joined them at the back door to the store.

"We'll keep this between us," he told Zeke and the girls. "I don't want no trouble with your Pa, but I think you're doing the right thing."

"Thank you, Sir," Zeke replied.

"Well, and besides, there's rumors about that the war's coming back this way later this summer. It's a good idea to get these little 'un's away, somewhere safe, before all that starts up again."

"Oh!" Zeke replied, surprised at that piece of war gossip. But at the moment the war was the least of his concerns.

Lighting a kerosene lamp, Mr. Bode led the girls to the ladies' section. He quickly found them each a dress and a warm jacket. Then he got them each a set of long underwear and heavy socks not only to keep their feet warm, but also to protect them from the new shoes that he slipped onto their feet. Both girls looked at Zeke as if to say, "Do we have to wear these?" He just smiled at them and nodded.

Pulling out the money left from his final Army check, Zeke told Mr. Bode, "I really need to get more food, enough to last us a few days anyway. I still have some of my final payment from the army. It's U. S. money, so it should still be good."

Mr. Bode headed to his grocery shelves and found several items which he stacked on the counter for Zeke to push into his rucksack. Zeke paid him, then he held out his hand.

"Thank you, Sir, for helping us. We may never see you again, but we'll never forget your kindness. We'll be gone so you can get back upstairs and forget you ever saw us tonight."

"That I will do, Zeke," Mr. Bode replied, shaking the outstretched hand. "You take care, and keep them safe."

"I'll do my best. There's one more thing, and this should be kept between us. I want someone to know where we've gone, just in case my sister or brothers come back looking for us. Tell them to go to the Cherokee town of Tahlequah. I'm hoping to stay in that area. Don't ever let Pa find out though."

Mr. Bode nodded, and Zeke took each girl by a hand as they left, disappearing into the darkness.

"So Mr. Humphrey, I brought them here. I knew where to go because Josie and Melly were always talking about going back home, where it was, what it was like. I thought we could take care of the place and have a roof over our heads until they came back from their hiding place. I'm hoping Mr. Ballew will have work for me to do so we can still stay around"

"That's quite a story," Andy told him. "I can't answer for Levi and Addie, but you stay put until I get back with them. I'll let them know that you're here, then Levi can give you an answer."

CHAPTER 27

LOOKING AHEAD

Late April, 1864

Addie sat in the darkness on the front steps of her home, chin resting on her knees with her arms wrapped around her shins. She stared into the star splattered sky, scarcely aware of the awakening sounds of the spring evening around her. Levi stood in the open door for a moment then walked over and sat down beside her. The children had taken the remains of the quilts from the cave and made beds to sleep on, and Andy had fallen asleep on the floor close to the smoldering coals in the fireplace with his head resting on Stirrup's saddle blanket. Zeke had taken his sisters to the loft where they had bedded down for the night.

"What are you thinking, Addie?" Levi asked his wife.

"When do you start to die?" she replied.

"What do you mean?" he replied, startled at the question. "I don't understand!"

"Is it when you begin to realize that nothing you do, or have ever done, really matters, nothing will really last, is that when you give up hope?" she said. "Years ago, when I was a child, all I wanted was get an education so I could be a teacher. I saved every penny I earned to buy books so I could learn everything possible. And I did it, I became a teacher, and I built a good little library in the process. Then I had to make a decision between marrying you or teaching, so I quit teaching. But I still had my home and family and little library, at least until now. I know most of that is still here, but nothing seems safe, nothing seems secure anymore."

She paused, hesitated, then continued.

"And you, Levi. All you wanted was to have your own cattle, your own ranch. You worked as a carpenter and a ranch hand for years, saving everything you could until you claimed this land and bought your first cow. You finally got a good herd, and you built this home, and barn, and buildings for us. You even made the furniture so we could eat as a family around a dining table. We had beds so we could sleep off the floor away from vermin, and chairs to sit in the evening while we visit or do our handwork. Now look. The furniture is gone, the outbuildings are in disrepair, only one cow left. All that effort. All those dreams."

Levi sat speechless, unable to respond. He sat in the quiet of the evening, thinking, until he felt he could reply to Addie's pessimistic words.

"Addie," he said, "We aren't very old before we start to learn about death, to know we won't live forever. So there's no sense in expecting eternal life. And the things we have? Well, that's all they are—things. It's what we put in our hearts and minds that stays with us over the long haul. No one can take away the knowledge you have or your love of learning, and they can't take away my love of working with cattle, living off the land. I guess the best we can do is hope is to get to the end of this life and be able to say we'd made it without intentionally hurting anyone. We can leave things in at least as good a shape as they were when we arrived. If we've known true love, had loyal friends, and are respected within the community, well, seems to me we could say we did it right.

"All this?" he questioned with a wide sweep of his arm. "This just shows what little control we really have over this old world. The only thing we can control is how we respond to it. This is how I plan to respond. I'm going to shout 'We're back!' then go out and start to rebuild. We'll make another good life for the children, encourage them to live right, learn what they can, and become independent adults. That's pretty much what we humans do. Everything else, well, that's just like dandelion fluff. It can be blown away with the puff of a breeze."

Addie sighed deeply then turned to Levi and grinned. "I knew I liked you for some reason. You've got more sense than any other ten men I've ever known!" And she slipped under his arm, her head resting on his chest.

1865

CHAPTER 28

LOOKING BACK

JULY 1865

Sounds of wagon wheels crunching across gravel carried through dense underbrush to the cabin that sat where the trail dipped below the hill. Addie knew within minutes she would hear sounds of horses' hooves and the squeaking of leather saddles of mounted riders as the wagon approached. A quick glance at Josie and nods to Evan and Humphrey sent the children out the back door.

Evan and Humphrey dashed to the barn yelling at the top of their lungs, "They're here! Papa, they're here."

Levi stepped from behind the door of the barn and waved at his sons, signaling that he had heard them and would be up to the house as quickly as possible. The boys raced around to the front porch and stood with Josie until the wagon came into sight.

Meantime Addie wiped her hands on her apron and pulled her long brown hair into a fresh bun. She untied the apron and laid it across the back of a chair. She left the outdoor cook shack that Levi had built behind the house to keep the heat of the cast iron stove outside and joined the children on the porch just as the wagon turned the corner. They all began waving. Aelie and Hazel were on the front seat with Jackson between them holding the reins in his hands. Zeke rode next to them on the horse called Stirrup, and Andy brought up the rear.

Within moments the horses were tethered to the hitching post by the front gate. Aelie reached for Andy's hand, and he helped her step down from the wagon. As he offered his hand to his daughter, Addie walked to Aelie's side and gave her a tender hug.

"It is so good to see you, Aelie. We weren't sure if you'd still be able to make the trip out here from town," she said. Addie then turned to Hazel and gave her niece a hug as well.

"This trip may be my last for awhile," Aelie replied with a smile. She continued softly, "You may notice how big I have gotten for only five months. My sister says she thinks I may be carrying two babies, twins like Jackson and William."

"Oh Aelie, twice the fun, but twice the work as well!" Addie exclaimed.

"Yes, but Jackson is proving to be wonderful help, and I think he'll be a great father. My sister, Paralee, is going to live with us since her family is all gone. It will be good for her and a great help for me."

Andy, Zeke, and the boys quickly unloaded the sacks of flour and sugar, tins of baking soda and powder and other supplies Andy had brought from town. Jackson slipped a small, tightly wrapped package into Nicholas's hand

"After dinner!" he whispered.

Nicholas quickly unwrapped the paper and exclaimed, "Candy! Hard candy! We haven't had any since, well, since I don't remember when. Yummy." Then Jackson climbed back on the wagon and urged the team forward, following the tracks that led behind the house. Andy and Zeke followed with their horses as the men headed to the barn to tend to the animals

Addie lead Aelie up the steps to a cane back chair on the porch. She, Hazel, and Josie took nearby chairs, then they visited while they all enjoyed the cool breeze that drifted across the shaded spot.

"This reminds me of the weather at Jackson's and my wedding last summer," Aelie commented, "fairly warm, but not too terribly hot." She paused a moment and added, "Sometimes I'm still amazed by the idea he wanted to marry me."

"Oh, Aelie, why?" Addie responded.

Aelie smiled and answered, "Well, first, I'm blind. I'm almost 4 years older than Jackson, and I'm a full blood Cherokee."

Addie thought for a moment before she replied. "Aelie, as he is your eyes in your darkness, you are his crutch when he stumbles. Four years isn't that much difference in your ages, and our family has always had bonds with the Cherokee. Besides all that, you a beautiful woman!"

"*Wa'-do*," Aelie replied. "You are kind to make me feel so welcome in your family."

Josie turned to Hazel and asked, "How are things going with the mercantile? I'm so glad Uncle Andy was able to get it rebuilt so quickly, but is he still having problems getting things stocked?"

"Yes, some," her cousin replied. "But since the war is officially over I think we'll see things easier to come by."

"Okay, I have a nosy question. How did he do it, I mean, how could he afford to buy what he needed to even get started over again?"

Hazel laughed. "Well, he has Grandfather Price to thank for a lot of that. Early in the war, when we first started talking about going to Texas, Grandfather gave him some advice, surprisingly good financial advice coming from a preacher. He told him to take his funds out of that bank in Georgia where Father had continued doing business even after Grandpa Humphrey died. Grandfather Price told him he also needed to take his money out of the bank in Tahlequah and to exchange his paper money for gold. It was a smart move although at the time it seemed like he might be losing some value in the trade. Father decided how much we might need to take with us when we left for Texas, and he buried the rest."

"Buried it? Where did he bury gold so it'd be safe?" Josie asked.

"Well, you remember your mother's family talking about their dog Lady, the one who tried to save your Aunt Desi from the rabid skunk? When they had to kill Lady because she'd been bitten, they gave her a doggie funeral and buried her. Papa went to that burial spot and dug a hole, and that's where he put the gold. He told us kids and Mama it was buried 'Where the Lady sleeps'. He left it to us to figure out what he meant if something happened to him. But when we came back from Texas, he had money, gold, left to get back on his feet."

Addie interrupted their conversation. "Excuse me, Hazel, but I don't want to bring this up with Andy until I'm sure it's a safe topic. Have you heard from Annie and the children lately?"

Hazel nodded. "They've managed to get a few letters back to us from the wagon train. Mama seems to have gotten over being angry at me for not going with them. The first letters came to me before I left Mount Tabor with the Pettit family to come home. Now they come to Father here when someone is coming back east and is willing to bring them. The Butterfield Trail Stagecoach Line used to come this way from where they are, but there were so many robberies and attacks on the coaches that they closed it back in '61."

She paused a moment before continuing. "The last post was from a town called Tucson on what they call the Gila Trail not far from the Mexican border. William said it was terribly hot there even thought it was still spring, but it wasn't too far on to California so they may be there by now."

"How about your mother and Delphia?" Addie asked.

"Mother seems to have had second thoughts about leaving Father like she did, but she still feels her place is with William right now. As for Del, she seems to be the kind of plant that blossoms wherever she's planted."

"Is William still having problems?"

"Not as bad as before. Mother says he's sleeping better, not having nightmares as often as he was, but he still has times when he is despondent and shuts himself away from everyone. The thing that seems to affect him most is sudden loud noises. That causes him to go into a panic, and it takes awhile for him to calm down." Hazel paused again, then added, "I hope he can find his balance in California, and then they can all come back here now the war is over. Perhaps life will get back to some kind of normal after awhile."

Josie looked at her mother behind Hazel's back, grinning, and winked. Then she asked her cousin, "How is Zeke getting along? Is his job with Uncle Andy working out?"

Hazel blushed and ducked her head. "Oh yes," she replied. "He's doing a wonderful job. Father couldn't have found a better employee to help him. He just works so hard. Sometimes he comes to our house for dinner. And he has even gone to church services with us."

"Hummmm . . . ." Addie said. "It sounds like he might be doing a little courting," and she smiled at her niece.

"Oh, no!" Hazel exclaimed. "We're too young, but Father said in another year it would be okay. That is, if it's okay with me. And I think it will be," she finished with a smile.

They entered the house as Melly, Susie, and Zelma clambered down the stairs from the attic.

"Hello, Hazel and Aelie," Melly said. Susie wiggled her fingers in greeting, and Zelma ducked her head acknowledging their presence. "Mother, what can we do to help with dinner?" Melly asked.

"You girls go down to the spring house and bring back that crock of milk and the butter. Be careful and don't spill the milk or you won't have any to drink with your meal," her mother instructed. The girls walked out of the door then raced out of the yard and down the hill toward the spring.

"How is Zelma doing?" Hazel asked.

"Much better," Addie replied. "She talks some now and seems to have gotten over most of her nervousness about being around people. We're all careful not to make her think we're raising a hand to her. That really frightens her. I guess her father was just pretty horrible, but thanks to Zeke she's out of that situation for good."

"What do you hear from Zena?" Josie asked.

"She's doing well. She knows you wanted her to stay here, but she wanted to be near Zeke. Having her work for the Downings while Zeke is helping Father has been a good arrangement. They treat her kindly, almost more like family than a housemaid. They've even allowed her to come to the classes I've been having in the back of Father's store. I have nine children in class now, and I hope Tahlequah will be reopening their schools in a year or so. There is a possibility I might get a real teaching position then."

Just then Levi, accompanied by Jackson, Andy, Zeke, and the boys came stomping in the back door.

"Dinner ready yet?" Andy asked.

"Have you heard the dinner bell?" Addie replied with a smile.

"Well, no," he said sheepishly. "We'll just sit and wait like the gentlemen we are, right fellas?" They scattered about the living room taking advantage of the breeze coming through the open windows and front door.

"Did you hear that Watie finally surrendered?" Andy asked Levi.

"Yes, but several weeks late! Seems he didn't get the message that the rest of the South had given up. Really sad about Lincoln. Not to say I agreed with all his politics, but I think things might have gone smoother now the was is over if he hadn't been assassinated."

"Hopefully the Union will let the Indian Nations go back to governing themselves, and the states will just take care of putting themselves back together. But somehow I don't have much faith in that happening," Andy added.

Within a few minutes the jingle of the dinner bell sounded from the kitchen, and the gentlemen rose to take their places around the kitchen table. In the center was a wild turkey Humphrey had shot, and Addie had baked to a rich golden brown. Next to it was a large platter of crisp fried catfish Evan and Nicholas had caught that morning. A round yellow bowl of succotash made from corn, lima beans, squash and peppers from their own garden sat on one end of the table. Melly and Zelma had brought up a basketful of watercress from the spring, and after they cleaned it Addie tossed the tiny leaves with a thinly sliced cucumber and sprinkled the salad with dill seed.

She scattered bacon bits over the mixture then poured the hot bacon grease over the leaves to wilt them. The wilted salad was placed next to another bowl that was filled with new potatoes and green beans, and a platter stacked with sliced cornbread was placed close at hand. A fresh blackberry cobbler was cooling on the stove in the outdoor cooking shack. Smiling in satisfaction, Addie surveyed the bounty spread before them and recalled the months of near starvation in Minaw's Cave.

Andy offered a brief prayer, then Levi spoke to those gathered around his table.

"Every one of you has been a blessing in my life. We don't know what lies ahead as the Cherokee Nation and the United States recover from this long and devastating war, but we can be thankful we have each other, have known each other, and have had the opportunity to help and be helped by each other. These may be the greatest gifts we ever receive. In past months we have known what it is to be hungry, but now we have this feast on the table in front of us. Dear friends and family, let's eat!"